I0746858

This Book is a work of fiction.

All of the characters, organizations, and events portrayed in the novel are either products of the authors imagination or are used fictitiously. Its not about you.

THIEF OF FAE

THESE HALLOWED HILLS SERIES

Quick Quill Publishing © 2022

Also by S.L. Mason

THESE HALLOWED HILLS

TRICK OF FAE

TEST OF FAE

THORNS OF FAE

TWIST OF FAE

TRAITS OF FAE

THIEF OF FAE

TEMPEST OF FAE

DEDICATION

~ 5 ~

To SurfBreak Café in Honomu Hawaii and Malissa without

your coffee I might not have made it, and for all the meals I

would otherwise have missed.

Thank you

TABLE OF CONTENTS

~ 9 ~

CHAPTER 1

MERCIA

No matter where I stood, the wake lines of Fadmor's CB pushed at me. His mother never wanted someone like me here. Her spells blocked the entrances. They were like a layered cake from the world before the fall, each song, building on the old, mixing together and growing stronger with each application.

However, I was stuck here. I couldn't leave.

Not yet.

I was still getting used to the new me, the me that I was meant to be.

Before Puca forced momma to change me. Before Puca tricked me.

The scent of cologne and something else laced the air, but I refused to acknowledge the person who wore it.

"Mercia, you have to talk to me," Nick whispered, and the heat from his body warmed my skin. The roof I was standing on was cold and watching for Govs was lonely icy work.

"No, I don't. I don't have to look at your lying face either," I retorted even though I wanted to sink into the warmth he offered, to give in to the fire that raced over me when I was with him.

Or the way he kissed me.

But that fire quickly became a cold, wet shower when the truth drenched me. He was Puca's son. He was there when Puca extracted my oath. He watched me my whole life and never lifted a finger.

Why?

My jaw worked the muscle over the bone.

"Fae has rules. I was only following them." His voice rose enough to carry. It was as if he could hear the thoughts marching around inside my head. They were ants, and their little feet itched as they trod all the crevasses between the gray matter.

I turned and caught a glimpse of him running his fingers through his hair, the same way his father did. I gritted my teeth. He then tucked his hands under his biceps in his typical Nick fashion.

"Yeah? Did the rules say to let me almost die? Or the need to hide who your father was? Would my father have done that?" I threw in the last part to hurt him. I didn't know what my father would do. For me, Arty was nothing more than a mysterious name from the past.

"Arty would have never left your side. Ever." He looked down at the cracked black tar paper covering the roof. There were once rocks here, but they were gone now. "The humans had to believe you were one of them. I don't look human and haven't for a long time. It wouldn't have worked."

I didn't say a thing.

"God damn it, Mercia!" He grabbed my arm and pulled me around to look at him.

His moss-green eyes smothered me with the Fae fire burning behind them. "I should have told you sooner, but they had you, and you were going to die. I couldn't let that happen. I - I... you know how I feel about you." He finished, his voice thick with emotion. His lips were so close to mine. I wanted to lean in and…

I pulled my pounding heart away from its desire and turned back to watch the CB's perimeter. "I'm on watch. I don't have time for liars." I glanced back at him, keeping my face blank and my lips tightly together.

Control, hunters have control.

I needed to keep that veil of control over my actions.

"I can't say what a human would, you know that," he whispered, "All I can do is use my actions to prove to you that you're wrong." He moved into my line of sight.

"Good luck with that," I calmly replied.

The alley on this side of the CB was quiet. It was not the most likely approach for an attack. Yet, I shifted my eyes left and right, looking for it anyway. I had to, to keep myself from looking at him.

"I don't need luck." His Fae marked hand brushed my cheek before he walked away, leaving the scent of his cologne behind and me with tears in my eyes.

How do humans do this?

The truth was, and I didn't even know if I wanted to face the truth, I was angry.

Angry!

I didn't remember anything about the day momma died.

Angry!

Larka and the Govs had Ron.

I'm enraged!

Cassidy had my crossbow. Plus, a long list of other things.

But mostly, I was angry that Nick left out the most important piece of information about himself.

Parentage.

If I was being fair, I always left that part out as well. Ron didn't know anything about my family other than they were dead.

Until a few days ago...

I wouldn't have cared that Nick's father was Fae. It was because of who his father was.

Puca - the most troublesome Fae alive.

He spread chaos to everything he touched.

"You can punish him forever." Puca's comment broke into my thoughts, grating over my already raw nerves. The scent of horse and leather always followed the one-time king.

"Yep, that's the beauty of Fae. We can really carry a grudge into the next millennium. We know how to hate," I replied in a dry voice that puffed out warm mist into the frigid air.

"Or you could turn his infatuation to your advantage," he said, shuffling his feet across the rooftop.

"More of your manipulating advice?" My eyes shift from one end of the alleyway to the other.

"No, yes, maybe," he chuckled to himself, before the laugh came to an abrupt end. "Where is the stone bowl and the wand of Danu, Keeper?"

My head whipped around to stare at him. "Safe." I narrowed my eyes and took him in.

"I'm afraid that isn't enough to appease me anymore. My magic tells me that may not be true." He stared me down with his thumbs locked in the belt loops at his waist.

Snow drifts were pushed up on the sides of the roof, leaving brown and black muddy puddles to melt and refreeze. Yet, Puca stood in the freezing cold with no shirt. I couldn't even tell if it affected him in the least.

I guess that's what gets me the most.

"Isn't it a bit nipply out here even for you?" I asked and went back to watching the alley.

"No, don't change the subject. Where are they?" he demanded. Puca's ability to manipulate his voice wasn't just for tone. It was laced with compulsion.

"You swore to help. Now help! Take me to the one weapon no Fae or human should ever hold!" Puca ordered.

"I'm on watch. I can't leave," I supplied without taking my eyes from the alley.

Puca's scent dispersed only to be joined by a new one.

"Robin sent me to relieve you." The girl said while rubbing her hand over her rump.

I hitch a half-smile and shrug. Puca always gets his way.

CHAPTER 2

SARAH

The cold stone of my seat chafed my ass and I did my best not to fidget. Fae milled around, whispering to each other and glancing my way. Janice was close. I could call an end to court and retire to my rooms or walk the garden. Yet, none of that was enough for me.

I was trapped here and I hated it. If I wanted to survive, I needed to embrace it, to love it. I didn't and I was not sure I ever would.

"My Queen, there is a matter we need to handle," Finian murmured in my ear.

I heaved a sigh and gave him a slight nod of acknowledgment.

More shit to deal with.

Part of me wanted to pinch the bridge of my nose while another part wanted to scream. Finian was a good seneschal, and I only chose him to keep an eye on him.

Janice and Nick were of the same mind - don't trust Deston, or his brother. Deston left Finian to rot in an iron room. That was enough to ensure that his loyalty should lie with whoever freed him.

Shouldn't it?

I glanced over at Janice and he, in turn, announced the end of court.

My wings beat down and I rose up in the light air that moved with me. It was more like a floating feather catching an upward breeze than flying. It still gave me a thrill and fear. At least now I didn't lurch one way or the other when I moved.

Control is the key to anything.

I kept telling myself that, hoping it will become true.

Control your wings, control the realm, control your feelings, control your Fae.

It was a big jumbled mess of strings. If I pulled the wrong one, the whole lot would pounce on me.

I glanced over at the few Fae still in the throne room, the tops of their heads exposed to my whims. I snapped my fingers, turned and left the room. Finian and Janice followed me down the hall to my private office.

I took my seat at my desk and waited for one of them to speak.

"Most of Jacques' holdings lay dormant, awaiting a new lord. The magic runs wyld. It is attacking any Fae that ventures into his old lands." Finian left the solution hanging in the air. I hate being led. I wished he would come right out and tell me what he wanted.

I drummed my fingers on the desk. Puca was right from the get go - *the best leaders listen and wait; the answer will present itself.*

So, I waited.

"I think it needs a new lord to rule it," he finally sputtered.

"Who do you purpose to be granted this honor?" Janice inquired with both arms crossed. His violet eyes burned into Finian's head, but Finian never gave him a side glance.

"I do not know. I was locked away for some time, as you know, cousin. Deston meant to kill me. And, apparently, you too. You only stand here today because I extracted an oath from him." Finian turned to face his cousin.

"What was that oath exactly? Not to kill me, or to let me live? No one can attest to this supposed oath. I know your brother as well. He would never have promised anything without something in return," Janice hissed. His stance was ready for a fight. The slight bend in the knees and the positioning of the feet turning his body slightly to the side. His hand wasn't on his sword, but in a flash, it would be.

Ever since Finian came out of Deston's dungeon with Nick and Arty, the two of them were at each other's throats.

"I thought you two were friends once." I intervened for the millionth time.

"I can't be friends with family members that keep secrets from me," Janice flashed me a glance, then moved his full attention back to his cousin.

"I have not lied to you, cousin. Deston was hell-bent on ridding himself of you. He knew you feared the next Queens' search. My love for you caused me to extract an oath from him. There was nothing more to it. Why can't you take me at my word? Why must we quarrel over this trifle?" Finian reached out his hand as a peace offering. Janice clenched his jaw and tightened his fingers into a fist.

"I can taste the lies coming from your tongue. They are laced with honey and the seeds of an apple, sweet and carrying a poison that kills." Janice gave me a hard stare and left the room, slamming the door behind him.

I wanted to follow, but Finian was right about Jacques' land running wyld. I had to put a stop to it. The entire area was being overrun by pixies, which were eating anyone who drew near the boundary. The land was thirsty for a new lord.

And one must be provided.

"Bring forth Cernunnos! Tell my father to attend me at court," I replied.

"You wish to make him a prince again?" Finian asked without bowing his head. He moved closer to my desk and my side, then kneeled down in supplication.

"My Queen, that portion of land requires an UnSeelie to rule. It will suffer no other." He stared up at me with his aquamarine blue eyes. For a moment, I was entranced. The feeling of floating in an ocean overwhelmed me.

He reached out as if to touch my hand, but the moment popped like bubble gum filled with too much air.

I pulled back, "Your charisma will not work on me, Finian," I reached for the power of air and slammed him against the wall. "You've got a set of brass ones. Get the fuck out of my office! Send for my father and be thankful I don't throw you in an iron room myself for your shit!" I screamed, then pushed him out the door into the wall in the hall.

He slumped to the floor, then quickly found his feet. He dusted himself off and crossed his fingers along his arm over his chest, before tilting his head down.

I wasn't going to be mollified with his stupid Fae motions. I slammed the door and rubbed the bridge of my nose.

It's always like this.

The fight was there just under the surface.

Why can't it be easy? Just once!

What had Deston said? Was it that his brother had charisma, and that it was strong? I huffed at the thought of Deston and his tricks.

Ugh! And the gross way he kissed me.

Even now, I wanted to wash my mouth out after retching. I ran my hand down my neck as if to push the vitriol back down. Other than Janice and Nick, I didn't have friends here. And Nick was always gone these days, watching over Arty's kid.

The walls began to water with my unshed tears. Arty was dead for a long time now, yet, for me, it happened just a few months ago. The ache of his loss pushed at me. My thoughts trailed around the room until I found what I was looking for, Arty's glasses and his cellphone. I itched to power up the phone and watch him, living in those moments for just a little while, dreaming that none of this ever happened.

I closed my eyes and counted to ten.

It's all the time I can give myself.

I stood and moved to find Janice, smoothing his ruffled feathers.

The violet trail of Janice's magic led me to a war room. Janice was inside, beating the crap out of some poor Fae trainee.

"If you want a fight, I can give you a battle," I offered and leaned against the wall to watch him, tucking my wings in tight to my body.

"I have no wish to fight you, my love." He released the male, allowing him to drop to the floor before offering him a hand up.

I waved the Fae away, and he quickly departed the room. The doors sealed behind him.

"Why do you fight with Finian?" I asked, trying not to turn it into a fight between us.

"He's lying about something. I know it." Janice moved to my side and pulled my hand to his lips. My pulse jumped, and my mouth grew dry a second before he pulled me in and devoured me with his kisses. I allowed my tongue to war with his as my hands moved freely over his body.

Janice trailed kisses down my neck, talking between each one. "He wishes to steal you away from me. I can see that."

Panting, I released a giggle, "That's stupid, and even if he did, it wouldn't work. I Love. You," I moaned, then snapped my fingers to remove all our clothes, showing him how stupid an idea it was.

Janice pulled back, "A consort is replaceable. He will find a way. My cousins will never back down." He leaned his forehead against mine a moment before he seized my lips.

"One is locked for all time by a crown, and the other is too weak to take me," I murmured over his skin.

Janice laced his fingers through my hair and wrenched my head back, "Don't believe all you see, my love. They will trick you in any way they can." His lips found mine and tore them apart.

I pulled back, "Explain! And enough with the sexy shit," I growled. No matter how much I wanted him, I needed his knowledge more.

I hate this shit!

I couldn't give myself over to my feelings. Ever! There was a fight, and I had to face it head-on. I pushed my desires into a little glass bottle and tossed it into a box along with all the other feelings I didn't have time for, at the bottom of my psyche.

Janice stepped away, "Finian and Deston are twins born of the same chrysalis. They have always worked in congress. His motives will always be suspect. I can't stress enough how lightly you should tread," he stopped talking and paced the room. I watched with hooded eyes, hoping to hide my hunger for the information he held.

"I love you, and nothing will ever change that." He heaved a deep breath, "You are my Queen, my sexual partner, and the Mother of all Fae. Without you, all of Fae will fade into nothingness." He broke off and searched the floor for other flowery things to slather over me.

"Stop! I can't stand the surgery coating." I rolled my eyes and walked away. "I hate having Fae sunshine up my ass. Can't you give it to me straight without all the extra shit?" I groaned.

"Finian is a wolf in Fae's clothing. If you continue to trust him, I will be forced to leave the castle and find service in one of the courts." Janice's words were clear and without emotion. He didn't look away or attempt any subterfuge. His magic waked with determination, and the violet lines were flat.

Air hitched in my chest.

Would he really leave me?

"You aren't serious," I whispered.

"As moss grows in moist shade and water flows to lower terrain. If you don't heed my council, then you have no need for it,." he hummed under his breath as his clothes flew to his outstretched arms. The fabric slipped over his body.

I snapped my fingers, and my clothes reappeared on my flesh. The room grew cold, and the cloth did nothing to fight back the frigid edge.

"Get rid of him! Give him his brother's land, give him to your father to kick around. Cernunnos would enjoy abusing one of Jacques' minions. But do not allow him to stay here as one of your trusted intimates," he growled.

My dry mouth found no words with which to respond. Janice bowed stiffly to me and went to the door. He waited for a moment before throwing a glance over his shoulder. He couldn't unlock the door. My magic was too strong for him to counter.

I waved two fingers in the air with a hum and released the mechanism. He yanked the door open and stormed out.

I screamed while pounding my fists into the floor I'd fallen on.

Why? Why can't it be easy?

I should be a freshman in college, working on my freshman fifteen at the nearest keg party, not walking the tightrope of Fae politics and hoping to come out on top, my only alternative being death.

Existing in Fae had more in common with the medical warning label for medicine. The side effects were loss of appetite, may cause sleeplessness, consulting with someone if symptoms persisted, chest and ass pain are normal, and my favorite one, and/or death. Every medicine label says and/or death. Dealing with the Fae was no different, you could magically be cured and/or dead.

I took to my feet and whistled the door open with a slam, stepping out into the hallway, on a mission heading for the throne room. I made it two steps only to be hit with a blast of magic. My body lifted into the air, and my feet floated in front of me as I was pushed fifteen feet down the hall. The puppet on a string effect enveloped me. The kinetic energy from the blast lessened, and I slammed into the floor.

I landed with a crack that rang through my brain. My head pounded in time with my beating heart, and my eyesight blurred.

Janice's face danced around my mind before darkness engulfed my world the same way Fae had.

CHAPTER 3

MERCIA

I took the stairs slow and steady. Puca didn't like to wait, but I had no fucks left to give. The musky scent of leather followed me, along with an exasperated sigh. At the bottom, I turned left and headed to my room.

Keeping my footsteps even, I ambled the well-worn path. Fadmor was generous. A room of my own was more than I could ask for.

There must be a price.

Fadmor would want something. It was the Fae way, and Fadmor was Fae. He didn't need to admit it for it to be true.

A portal ripped through the fabric of the hallway, tearing it in half. Puca stepped out before me.

"How do you always get right in my way?" I demanded. Puca's uncovered chest irritated me. I didn't know if he didn't feel the cold or he just liked to show off.

"As I remember it, I was called the last few times," Puca remarked, then offered me his hand, which I ignored.

"I have never called you," I remarked and stepped around him.

"Mercia, I helped birth you. I have watched over you your entire life. I am not in your way. I am your ally," he stated and moved in front of me. I huffed as my eyes shifted left and right, examining the floor to give me time to scrap together my answer.

"I don't remember you being there when I emerged from my chrysalis," I replied, and yanked open my bedroom door. Momma said, '*never let the past get in the way of the present.*'

What got in my way before, shouldn't get in my way now! Yet it did.

I hummed the lock off and waltzed to the bed, plopping down. I flung my feet up and crossed my ankles, leaning back into my pillow with my hands behind my head.

"Is this where the stone bowl resides?" Puca asked, running a finger along the wall before rubbing it to his thumb. He threw me a sour look and snapped the dirt away, leaving the walls clean.

"Nope," I said and closed my eyes. "It's not here. It's nowhere near here," I yawned as my limbs grew heavy with leathery.

The crack of leather split the air, and my eyes snapped open.

"Sing a song of sixpence, and wake yourself," Puca barked with elongated teeth. "I have no time for your hunter games. There is danger all around us, and you wish to sleep!" He growled.

The compulsion in his chiding forced me to my feet, and before I knew it, I was singing for sixpence.

"Why the sudden need for the bowl? Didn't I keep it safe all these years, keeping it and myself hidden?" I demanded with renewed vigor.

"The stakes have changed," Puca's voice grew dark, "We're in a race against time and the darkest Fae ever created." His body paced without moving as if his very skin prowled the room.

"What changed?" I inquired, holding my breath. I didn't know what I was holding it for, but a flavor lingered at the back of my throat. It tasted of coppery sugar, soon to become caramel with a little more heat.

I'd moved to my feet, holding a knife at the ready.

A knowing smile peeled across Puca's face. "You taste the hunt?" he stated, then pivoted on one foot to take me in. His eyes flashed red, revealing his animal side.

"There is a quest that must be fulfilled before you can track down our prey, little one." He smirked and slicked his black hair away from his face, his eyes sliding back from red to orange to yellow.

I huffed and moved away, but the beat of my heart still carried the rhythm of the hunt. It throbbed just under the surface and begged to be answered. I held the emotion taut as if it was a bowstring held tight, waiting for the perfect moment to be released.

The thrill of the hunt never had such a strong pull, but I haven't been this Fae before either.

"What quest?" I growled as the need to fulfill my role overwhelmed me.

"I have already told you what is required. Take my son and bring me the wand of Danu along with the stone bowl. Then and only then, will I give you a hunt for the ages. They will create new magic in your name," he mused and pivoted from one foot to the other with the twirl of a dancer.

Ugh!

I groaned. "Is this how you sucked my mother into your stupid plans? With promises of glory?" I turned my back on his visage. My human side scoffed at his lame enticements.

The humming in my veins beat a wardrum, and the desire to answer its call pummeled at me.

"Even now, your desire to track your prey eats at you," he whispered in my ear. The warm breath played over my hunter's senses, teasing me. "Take Nick! Complete this small matter, and move on to the challenge. You cannot deny what burns in your soul, hunter," his warm breath tickled my skin and raised my hackles.

Before I could gather myself, Puca whistled. The tune was similar to the one momma pounded into my psyche so many years ago, only deeper. Notes so low no one save a Fae could ever whistle its tune.

The freshly cleaned wall shivered and split. Nick stepped through the portal to stand before his sire.

Seeing them face to face made me realize both the differences and similarities. The eyes being the main difference. Pucas' were a canary yellow and cold, while Nick's were moss green and warm. Yet, they were both of a height and had black gleaming waves to their hair. Puca never wore a shirt, and as yet, I'd not seen Nick without one.

Nick's jaw clamped down, and the muscles worked over the bone. "You called," he grunted.

"Father. Call me by what I have earned," Puca patiently instructed.

Nick's nostrils flared, "Father."

I tore my eyes from the two Fae before me and crossed my arms, allowing my sight to trail everywhere but them until I spied a pair of boots dangling from Nick's fingers.

"My boots!" I spouted.

Nick's scowl turned into an easy smile as soon as he regarded me.

"The boots and your bag," he handed me my backpack.

I took both and inspected them for any damage. Part of me wanted to forgive him, but when I looked up to offer a form of thanks, Puca stood shadow over us, and I couldn't bring myself to do it.

"Your pains are noted," I replied, keeping my voice cool and even.

My fingers curled against my leg to hide my desire. The Fae form of thanks squeezed from my tongue like juice from a lemon. The scent was pleasing, but the taste bit and burned open wounds.

"Your shoes look much the same," Puca said and pranced around the room only to pivot on one foot, then turn and face me. His nervous dancing irritated me more than a toddler who shouts *'no'* at everything.

I stopped holding back, laced my boots on and glanced up. "Just because you got my boots back doesn't mean I believe you," I hissed and ran my hands down my torso to smooth my clothes.

"I didn't do this," Puca smiled, and his canary eyes twinkled in a knowing fashion.

I huffed.

Nick.

"Too bad my crossbow didn't make it too," I remarked and tossed the quiver from my bag on the bed.

In my mind's eye, I could see the decorative woodwork lining the side of momma's crossbow. I wanted to bite my lip, but I couldn't. That was a tell, and I couldn't give anything away. Puca would have noticed if I did.

When you're playing the grand game against a master, you can't stumble.

I reached inside and pulled out the rocks from my old room, then I rolled them around in my hand until a red stone reached the top of the pile. Internally, I heaved a sigh of relief. I tossed the rest of the rocks on my bed. Then, I threw the red stone at Puca, who caught it.

"There's your stone!" I said and crossed my arms and plopped down on my bed.

"That's why you wanted your things? You left the wand of Danu in the hands of the enemy?" Nick remarked, then ran his fingers through his hair, taking a step away.

He turned, ready to say something, but Puca raised his hand and silenced him.

"This is only part of the wand. Where is the rest? Puca demanded, then changed his mind, "The bowl, where is it?" He continued as hair raced over his face and down his chest. He bared his teeth, and they elongated, saliva dripping from the tips of his glossy canines. His nostrils flared as he huffed with rage.

Every bone in my body quivered in fear. I clenched my jaw down to keep my teeth from chattering.

"It's far from here," I whispered and took to my feet in an effort at bravado.

"Take me to it, Keeper!" Puca seethed. "I have no patience for your hunter games. Do not play them with me." Puca's growl reverberated around the room, and the wakes from his tone cut through me.

I squeaked in shock as the compulsion in his voice forced me to obey. I couldn't look away from him, but the magic wakes slammed me into the floor on my knees. I panted from the jarring pain, radiating up from my knee caps.

Nick placed his hand on Puca's arm, "Father, she will take you to it." His voice was calm.

I turned my head and snuck a glimpse at Puca and Nick. Nick, in turn, gazed at me and gave me a pleading stare. I gulped back, the fear clawing at my insides. I crossed my left arm over my chest, and laid crossed fingers over my breast bone, tilting my head down before touching my fingers to my forehead.

The act was enough to appease him. Puca's canine features faded away, leaving only Fae behind.

Inwardly, I breathed a sigh of relief, but my heart pounded with anger. He didn't need to abuse me to get his way.

I *was* dragging my feet. Puca's compulsion pulled back, allowing me to take to my full height.

I don't want to go back there.

Momma said that as long as we never went there, no one else would either. Her logic made sense to me. The only path to the stone bowl without me was by asking a flittermouse.

But humans don't talk to bats, and no other soul knows to speak to them but me.

"The state of Louisiana, in the hills," I said.

Puca looked at Nick and then back to me. "Take her and bring the stone bowl back with you."

I opened my mouth to protest, but a cold stare from Oberon froze the words on my tongue. Instead, I turned back to my bed and scooped up the rocks and tossed them back in my bag, pulling the quiver off of the bed and strapping it around my waist.

I slung my rifle over my shoulder and turned back to the two men. Puca sang a high song over me, one I'd never heard before. Instantly, my clothes changed with the enchantment.

"It will provide you with protection from the Govs weapons," he stated and turned back to Nick, nodding his head. He thrust his hand out and ripped a portal into the wall.

The sound of birds filtered in, and I stepped through to meet the forest on the other side.

If the stakes have changed, what changed them? And why are both the wand and the bowl so important to begin with?

CHAPTER 4

SARAH

The dayglow lights of Fae slowly filtered in under my closed eyelids. The effort to open my eyes was more than I could muster. The ringing in my ears was more of the high G bells rung by the fake Santas at Christmas time. It clawed at my mind.

I wanted to stop the sound, to destroy the person ringing the bell. I would have thrown every coin left in the world at them to make it stop. But the sound kept coming.

Finally, when I couldn't take it anymore, I screamed and sat up.

The source of the bell was actually my head, and the room was empty. Pain rushed to meet me. I cringed away from the dim light of Fae. My hands moved to hold my head only to encounter the broken tip on my crown. The hair on the back of my head was matted down, and bloody. The backside of my body ached.

The act of touching the wounds caused a fresh feeling to join the ringing - nausea. It roiled around from my head down to my belly, and saliva coated my throat. I leaned to the side and emptied the contents of my stomach onto the stone floor.

The room continued its spinning dance, and a new bout hit me hard and fast. I gripped the edge of the table, as my larynx joined the yak on the floor. I waited to see if my shoes would join the party.

Sweat covered my body. I panted to get rid of the horrid scent flooding the air. The walls rattled in an off-key. They didn't like me getting ill any more than I did. I laid my cheek on the cool table to ease the spinning and closed my eyes.

That was a big mistake.

A fresh round of nausea overran my senses, and I quickly opened my eyes to stop that march.

I hummed *light as a feather,* and sat up. I blinked to slow my eyes down and forced them to only focus on the wall before me.

The wall was covered in almond flowers. A few green fruits grew alongside the heady scented blooms. I loved the scent of almonds and hated the nuts. I whistled the noxious mess on the floor away, and the stone absorbed my one-time lunch. The room refreshed itself, leaving only the buttery scent of the almonds.

I blinked slowly and heaved a sigh. I sat up. I needed to reach the source of the explosion.

My wings pushed down and the lift moved me to the door. Without another thought, I hummed the door open. The poor thing slammed into the wall, rattling the other doors in the hallway. I whistled a high B flat to announce the opening of court.

I could barely keep my head from rolling around on my shoulders. My wings seemed to be the only thing keeping me moving. For the moment, I was glad to have them.

I turned my head to take in a Fae who darted into an alcove as I passed by. The tip of one of my wings was broken, hanging at an odd angle. My nostrils flared and burned.

What the fuck happened, and how long have I been asleep?

The stone throne loomed large through the main doors, while Fae milled around the audience chamber. The normal level of whispering was more of a loud shouting. The Fae weren't one for panic, but panic laced the air, giving everything the scent of saltpeter and sulfur.

I crinkled my nose, then erased the emotion from my face as one. The Fae turned to face me, bowing and curtsying in a wave. They were more like the wakes surrounding them. The fluid movement that only the Fae could engineer came as I entered the room and they parted, leaving me a path to the throne.

I stopped dead in my tracks. Other than the stone throne, there was nothing else in the room.

My kings were gone.

The anger blasted away from me, knocking Fae to the ground. The compulsion kept them in supplication.

"What is the meaning of this?" I demanded. The pounding in my head ratcheted up to a new decibel. The ring went from a bell to the high pitch whine of a radial arm saw cutting metal.

Other than the rustling of the walls, all was silent. No one met my eyes, or even attempted to glance up. Every head was bowed in fear.

The reason was obvious - the kings were gone. The blast was magic.

Only the breaking of a spell could create this level of mayhem.

The last time it happened, I'd taken my seat, changing the Fae realm for all time.

"Where is my consort and seneschal?" I inquired to the crowd of sycophants. I cocked an eyebrow as I moved. The flavor of distaste that lingered on my tongue resembled cream of tartar. It leavened the situation, causing it to rise. I moved deeper into the room to survey the outcome.

The stone throne was untouched. On the right-hand side a circle was burned into the floor, while the left-hand side was occupied by Deston's body.

He died still in the thrall of Wyld. His eye gazed unseeing at the ceiling, locked in the kaleidoscope of colors indicative of a full wyld possession. The leaves covering his torso were varying shades of orange, red and brown. The beauty of the colors was broken by a gaping hole in his chest cavity, leaving no doubts about his condition.

I always knew he was a heartless bastard.

But this was more proof than I needed.

Only the breaking of a spell could have caused the explosion I experienced. A magical rebound or the fulfillment of that spell. I sniffed the air, hoping a thread of the cause lingered. There were several magical remnants. One hung over Deston's body.

The Fae would snicker he never saw the end coming. Wyld takes your situational awareness away, leaving only the animalistic instinct to chase, hunt, rut, and eat.

The burned circle was a different story.

Just tilting my head to look down at what remained of Jacques put pressure on my frontal lobe and the nausea throb hit me again. There were no magic wakes, as the spell burned them away.

How am I to discover what happened with no trail?

I lifted my head and turned to take in the room, throwing off the malaise of my injuries.

There were no remains of Jacques, not even a ratty hair from his leg or a leaf that covered his chest. I'd expected Jacques to stand there for all time as an example to the others of what happens when you cross me. His demise was disappointing, to say the least.

There were no answers to my inquiries, just the quivering masses lining the walls. I turned and spit at the room.

"You spineless cowards! Which of you will stand and speak to your Queen?" I demanded, pushing the matted hair from my face. I must have looked as wyld as the corpse on the floor.

The voice came from behind me. "Only a prince would face the Queen in such a time, providing the information she wants," a woman stated.

I whorled around to face the Fae. Her indigo blue eyes glowed in the light in a way only a Fae's eyes could. She tilted her head down and crossed her arm and fingers before touching her head.

"Explain everything." I pointed to one of the guards. "Also, find my consort! Stop at nothing to bring him back to me. Tell him that I'm listening." It was my only way to say sorry without saying it.

I snapped a tracking spell for them to follow. The two Fae darted through the nearest archway, chasing after the violet trail.

The woman kneeled and bowed her head, making her black wavy hair enveloped her form.

"Rise!" I snapped since I didn't have time for the formalities or the patience.

"I am Mod, of the UnSeelie Autumn court. You will not find your seneschal here, and I know not of your consort." She stopped her narrow eyes shifting back and forth to take in the room for effect. "Finian freed his master."

The room gasped, as did I.

"What do you mean?" I growled. The nausea moved through my system with fresh vigor. I raised my hands and slapped them together to shut the murmuring mouths of the gathered fools.

"Finian is the sworn servant of Jacques. I was a witness to the oath many moons ago," she replied. She lifted her head to stare me down. She wanted to see if I would falter, but her deep indigo stare only shook my insides.

I mustered the strength and forced my body not to move.

Betrayal is a hard pill that should be swallowed dry. So you remember the feeling and never experience it again.

"How do I know you don't belong to him too?" I asked since the UnSeelie loved to play games.

She wanted something and was willing to step out of the Prince's shadow to get it.

Let's see how far she will go before she reveals her true intentions.

A smile played at the edge of her pouty lips. She looked more like a K-Pop singer than Fae any day of the week. Only the marking and ears gave her away. She could have passed on the surface all day long.

That is if she could walk in the daylight, which she can't.

"I will swear my lifelong allegiance to you, in return for Jacques Principality," she coolly replied.

My already swimming head threatened to pull me under. I gave myself one second to think about it over the high-pitched whining in my mind.

"Prove it.!" I said.

She kneeled at my feet and kissed the hem of my dress.

"I, Mod, daughter of Princess Fortia, the forest grower, do hereby swear my lifelong loyalty to Queen Sarinha, daughter of Allison and Cernunnos, grand-daughter of Puca Oberon the 1st and one time King of Fae and Demelza the fair," she stopped to look at me and I blinked back the pounding pain radiating from my body.

"Pledge your sword to any and all causes I deem necessary, never to oppose me in deed, or send another in your stead to oppose me. You will swear to be my tool as I see fit, until the magic takes you," I supplied and the broken tip of my wing throbbed.

I didn't just want her loyalty. I wanted it all. I wanted the very magic that fueled her life to be mine.

She swallowed, closed her mouth, then her tongue darted out to wet her lips. She repeated my demands, so I accepted her oath.

"I grant you the Principality once claimed by Jacques and rule over the Autumn court. As the first Princess in a thousand years, I order you to go locate Jacques. I want to know what he's up to, but I do not kill him." My head was beginning to sway, and dark spots loomed at the edges.

"It shall be as you say, my Queen." She left on her new quest. Her weeping willow dress brushed the floor as she swept from the room. The hush that held the court was released with her exit.

I snapped my fingers to end court and left. Only when I reached my personal chamber, I allowed myself to collapse on the floor. The walls reached for me and carried me to my bed, tucking the pussy-willow covers over my limp body. A Callalily dribbled water into my mouth. My kingdom offered me the succor my consort should have.

The tears came, but Janice did not. He was gone. I didn't listen to him, and he left just when I needed him most. I was too wrapped up in playing the game to see I was being played.

My lips trembled, then pierced for a moment. The desire to whistle for Nick came hard and fast. If I called, he'd come.

I can't.

The reality hit me hard - it would leave Arty's child alone and unprotected. I shoved my desperate wish away and blinked back the tears I shouldn't shed.

Mom.

She would come. But she couldn't protect herself, and I was too weak to protect her. Her magic couldn't heal me, as she wasn't Fae enough.

Wherever Puca put her, she should stay there.

His magic would keep her safe. Furthermore, just the fear of Puca was enough to keep others away.

Too bad that fear doesn't extend to me. No amount of fear will be enough to stop the onslaught for the throne.

I choked back the pain. I was alone for real this time. Before, it was easier. My unshakable belief that Arty was alive, kept me going. Arty was dead now. My mother brought me the news. Without Nick and Janice, I might never have left the stone throne. I would have wilted away, gripping the armrests.

Nick said he would never leave me down here. That was before he gave his word to keep Arty's daughter safe. It wasn't an oath, but close enough. I couldn't make him choose, it would twist him inside.

Janice was always there for me. He was the crutch I didn't want to admit I needed. Now that he was gone, I was floundering.

A rudderless ship.

And the truth of it squeezed my insides into a gooey mess. My head was light, and I couldn't tell if it was from the impact of the spell being broken, or my injuries.

Janice left me.

That only left Puca. Before I could wet my lips to whistle, the wall on the far side shivered and split. Puca stepped through the portal, and the room snapped back into shape. The scent of leather and man overran the space. The vice around my heart threatened to release the dam of pain and ask Puca to make it better. My eyes burned with the need to shed my tears and beg for help.

I can't! Puca wouldn't respect me if I did.

I pressed my trembling lips closed.

He kneeled down next to my bed, kissed my forehead and sang the physical pain away, leaving only my broken heart before disappearing never having spoken a word.

CHAPTER 5

MERCIA

Flittermice only came out at dusk. Then and only then would they begin their dance for food. Their leathery warm-blooded bodies winged between the trees, swooping and darting for the last of the insects out for a bedtime snack. I searched the dying light for my first friends, listening for the soft chirps they sent out, hunting the night skies for their prey.

Nick's breath came light and even over my shoulder. I lightly danced between the twigs and dry leaves in the silent movement of the hunt. It was a challenge I'd not faced since my emergence from the chrysalis, but one I enjoyed. The forest was an early friend. Momma and I'd played under the boughs for weeks, before heading to Lanta and the fight there.

Nick, too, seemed to know the movement of the trees and followed me soundlessly.

"Where are we going?" Nick asked in a voice so low you could mistake it for the groan of a branch.

I glanced at the shadowy bushes and underbrush for the telltale wakes of life, intelligent life. The forest gave back only the placid wakes of the undisturbed. I drank in the safety of it. I rarely found terrain so untouched and serene. It pulled at the edges of my psyche and eased the tight muscles of my back.

"To the bowl," I replied, then pressed my lips flat to keep anything else from slipping past my teeth. The less we said to each other, the better. Nick didn't deserve an explanation. I wasn't forever trapped in service to him, only to his father.

Just thinking about Puca Oberon turned my joy sour. A nostril curled up, and I bared my teeth. I swallowed back the growl that sat in the back of my throat. Nick wasn't that much different from me.

You can't control who your parents are.

That wasn't my problem with him. It was the lack of honesty. He lied by omission, and therein was the issue. He was more Fae than he was willing to admit. Holding back an important piece of the truth was a very Fae failing, one I too could claim.

But I never lied to Nick. After he kissed me, I would have told him anything he asked. The only holdback was the bowl and the wand. Those were not my secrets to share, and no amount of magic would have changed that.

A vow cannot be broken without consequence.

With magic, the price is high, so very high — death.

I hissed into the night to clear all thoughts of Nick's lies and Puca's tricks.

Crabgrass lined portions of the forest floor, the parts that sunlight reached. I searched the clumps for a long fat blade and plucked it from the ground. It pulled free and clear with a bowstring hum. I quickly positioned it in my hand and whistled into the sound pocket I'd created. What came out the other side was a flittermouse chirp.

It hit the magic waves around us and lit the forest up like daylight, daylight I would never see again. Puca had known the moment I made my choice, that avenue would disappear for me.

He never tells you the consequences of your choices.

I searched for the magic, waiting for the sound to bounce back. I held my breath, hoping one of my friends would answer my call. The reverberation came back with nothing amiss, only the sleeping forest and its many nocturnal residences.

I pulled in a deep breath and blew again, only longer, to extend the reach of the magical sonar. Nick's hand fell on my shoulder, and I shrugged it off. The wakes undulated away from us before returning with one chirp.

My feet sprinted in that direction, meeting grass and moss. My heart was beating to the rhythm of the wind, and I revealed myself in the chase. It was pure rapture. Finally, my flittering compatriot came into view. His swooping and diving whipped past my head, before coming to rest on my shoulder.

He crooned in my ear and clawed his way over my back and under my hair, then rested near my ear. I purred at the little rodent of the skies. His warm leathery body clung to me, and I petted him in reassurance.

I asked him about the forest and the secrets of the trees. His answer was filled with all I needed before he took flight again. His search for food was earnest; he had a family to feed. The flittermouse promised to meet me at the cave and brought a secret smile to my lips. Even in times like these, I still had friends on the surface.

"What did the rat with wings have to say?" Nick whispered. He was panting from the run, trying to keep up with me.

I stopped and turned to stare him down. "He said there is danger up ahead. Humans have taken over an old plantation house not far from where we are going. But the bowl is undisturbed. If we are lucky, we can be in and out in no time," I stated even though I couldn't help but feel disgusted.

How can he think so low of such a wonderful, loyal creature?

"Are you sure you can trust him?" he asked.

"Flittermice don't lie," I remarked. Maybe they did, but not the ones of this forest. My dig hit the spot.

Nick hung his head, then bent over to catch his breath. I hummed a light foot spell over his shoes to hasten his gate.

I don't need Puca's changeling slowing me down.

For a moment, I felt bad. Nick wasn't just any changeling. He was the Fae that saved me from certain death. He loved me. I had all the proof I needed on that end.

I'm alive.

I glanced up at him and gave him a small smile, keeping my teeth covered. I blinked to hide the emotion behind my gaze. Puca was right. I could punish him forever.

Right now — I can't forgive.

My heart wanted to, but my head said no.

Momma said to always listen to my head because hearts get led astray too easily. My internal war was nothing more than a distraction from the hunt.

Turning my eyes away from Nick's hungry ones, I focused instead on the forest.

I didn't remember a plantation around there, but yet again, I'd never traveled on this side of the forest. When we left the cave, we climbed the cliff face, and headed East to Lanta. Nick and I were coming from the West. I closed my eyes and tried to picture the map Momma showed me of America.

My name is in America.

I always thought that was funny. Even though I shared all the letters and some of the patterns, we sounded nothing alike. Momma named me after a kingdom that once existed before Britain was united.

Mercia was once the largest kingdom in Britain. It meant *"border people"*.

I am the border person.

I stood between Fae and the human world. Mercia was powerful and rich. Offa, one of the kings, made a deal with a Fae.

Momma.

Momma promised to help Offa defend Mercia from the other kingdoms, war being her favorite. However, he didn't ask for forever. When he died, Momma left, and Mercia was slowly cut up into pieces until there was nothing left. Momma gave me that name to remind me that you can't fight on too many fronts or borders. Also, because it meant *mercy* was in my name.

Show no mercy to your enemies, even if they beg please. For they will show you none.

I couldn't think of the great map's borders or the old names of places. The last time I saw it, I was so fresh from my chrysalis. It seemed a lifetime ago.

Before Momma died, before Puca, before Cassidy, and before Larka. Before Nick...

"Nick, we're in Louisiana. If we head South to skirt around the plantation, do you know what lies that way?" I asked, hopeful he had an answer that didn't resemble the one I didn't want to hear.

He stopped and turned to face me, then locked his hands under his biceps. "There is only one place South in Louisiana — New Orleans," he stated then scratched his chin as if to think.

The blood drained from my head, pooling in my shoes.

We couldn't go there. Not ever! The blood loss to my brain hit me as if a decrepit building had fallen down around me and left the blood high above my head. Momma made me promise. It wasn't an oath.

At least it wasn't that.

But it was enough to instill a deep-seated repulsion for the very name, let alone the place.

"Mercia," Nick asked concern lining his voice

The forest turned around me. I was trapped in a mental cyclone, weaving on my feet.

Nick wrapped his arms around me and pulled me in. "Baby, are you okay?" he rubbed his thumb across my cheeks.

I blinked to clear the fear that had overwhelmed me. I pulled back and stepped away to steady myself next to a tree. "We can't go there," I whispered, afraid to even say its name.

That city was pure evil. There were only three places Momma was adamant I never go and New Orleans was number one on that list. The other two paled in comparison. Savannah lost most of its power when Momma last visited. I would never cross an ocean, so the other one wasn't even worth thinking about.

"Well, there is a whole lot of water between us and New Orleans. I don't know of anywhere in Louisiana that isn't at or below sea level. The dikes are gone. That city has to be underwater and gone," he remarked. There was no fear in him. He didn't know what he was talking about. This was the human part of Nick talking. He wasn't thinking like a Fae. He didn't know what I knew. His memories of the past colored his response. All his time on the surface hadn't taken him there, and the memory of that city was a bubble of trapped time.

I pressed my lips tightly closed and shook my head. "There is one thing about New Orleans you've forgotten." I wanted to shake off this fear that had smoothed over me like a fine sheen of sweat. There was no way to do that.

If the plantation is North and New Orleans is south there is no safe passage.

Nick grabbed my arm and pulled me around to face him, "Yeah? Tell me then. What am I missing? Hurricane Katrina flattened that town, and the bombs from the fall finished it off," he shrugged.

"That city will never die, as the dead keep it alive," I groaned. The air to the North was cleaner than the air to the South and what little breeze still found its way under the trees moved that way.

Heading South with the wind at our back would announce our presence faster than a bat sign in the sky.

"You can't live if you're dead. You aren't making sense. Stop with the Fae games and spit it out!" he growled at me and for a moment, his hair seemed shaggy.

It was a trick of the forest light because just as fast as it came, the shaggy hair was gone.

I breathed out the word, "Witches." The hair on my arms stood on end, and a shiver ran across my skin. The forest grew still and quiet. The trees were listening to us.

"They are everywhere. It's not a problem," he replied, then ran his fingers through his hair, slicking the thick black curls to his neck. I'd seen his father do it a hundred times in the last few weeks.

It's a nervous tick.

Yet, not one Nick had before.

"These are different. They are powerful and have harnessed the power of the dead," I glanced over my shoulder, looking for the tell-tale signs of a familiar.

The wakes showed the area as clear. However, my hunter's senses told a different story. The forest had eyes and ears behind every leaf.

"We should go North, and chance the plantation." I nodded to reassure myself of the decision, and moved to fulfill it.

"Wait. Mer—" I locked my hand over his mouth and shook my head to quiet him.

"Don't say my name! There is power in a name." I pulled my hand back and checked my weapons. "They are listening. Trust me!"

Nick reached out as if to caress my cheek but curled his hand back into a fist, giving me a curt nod of acknowledgment. He pulled his gun from the holster it lived in and hummed over the weapon. The tune was a ditty I'd heard momma use - an Alice song.

Tweedle-dum and tweedle-dee, resolved to win a battle

For Tweedle-Dum and Tweedle-Dee, had a nice new set of arrows,

Just then, a monster flew by, and with one bolt, Dee took the beast down.

Which emboldened the heroes, they released the rest of their missiles to finish off the hostiles.

Momma said the Alice songs were good for small skirmishes. They were not for a long drawn-out battles and they were definitely not for a war.

Nick's choice was sound. I wondered who taught him the Alice songs?

It has to be Puca. After all, he made them just for her.

I had never met Alice. Momma didn't speak of the past. She only mentioned her in regards to magic and fighting.

Our path followed a game trail. I kept close to the track until I spied the first sign of humans.

It was a large branch that had been sawed off. The path was being cleared to extend deeper into the forest. I held my fist up to signal Nick to stop.

I pointed up to the trees and hummed light as a feather. We both chose a different tree and as quick as a chipmunk, we scurried, gripping the bark to leave no mark. I reached a high mark in the tree where the first split in the main trunk branched. It went two different directions - one pointed South, the other one North. I shot Nick a knowing look and moved North, tiptoeing along the heavy branch until it branched again.

We picked our way out to the thin weaker branches until the tree bowed under our weight. Weighing nothing more than a feather or the Spanish moss that clung to the trees. The tree was so thin it only held the leaves it grew.

I gauged the space between trees and leaped. The branch was thicker than the one before, and I followed it back to the trunk. Nick caught my eye and winked at me. I shook my head.

The snap of a twig and the russell of dry leaves brought us to a standstill in the canopy. My flittermouse friend winged back to me. He swooped and dove, forcing me back. His frantic chirps spoke of invaders and thieves.

Finally, I squatted on the branch and offered him my shoulder. The small body shivered with exhaustion, he smacked his lips, and I offered him a sip of water. The flittermouse slowly whispered *'Witches.'*

I took one look at Nick's questioning face and dove to the forest floor, rolling up onto my feet at contact. I sang for all the power I could muster and dashed. *Jack be nimble* danced over my lips three times. I layered the magic and gained speed with each iteration, my heart beating in time with the song. I leaped over downed trees and dodged the underbrush.

The fear that clenched my guts wouldn't release. I waited too long, and trusted the forest too much.

Damn those human half-breed mutts!

Witches were the bane of the surface. I pulled a sapling from the ground as I passed and quickly sang it into shape. I pulled a clump of hair from my head and wove it into a string adding strength with each fold of the braid. Finally, I strung the fresh bow with a whistle and a hum.

Whipping an arrow from my quiver, I knocked the bolt, ready to kill all I laid eyes upon.

CHAPTER 6

SARAH

Normally, after being healed, I was hungry. I'd eat anything in sight. This time, however, the thought of food did nothing more than turn my stomach into a cement block. I couldn't bring myself to replace the nutrients I'd used to fix my body.

Puca's repair couldn't fix what was broken inside. Plus, the invisible gaping hole in my chest ached. I couldn't feel my heart beating because it didn't. It bled. It was gone. Janice ripped it out and took it with him when he left.

A new understanding dawned on me.

Puca...no wonder no one can get close to him.

He and I were the same. I rubbed my aching sternum. Blinking back the tears I couldn't shed, I lifted my chin.

My fingers snapped the door open and my attendants entered. A few stared My recovery was obviously caused by magic. They shot furtive glances at each other under their lashes.

The question that hung in the air for them was just one - who had healed me? It was none of their business.

They can speculate until a new kingdom comes.

None needed to know it wasn't Janice. I hadn't asked Puca to heal me, and he'd asked nothing in return. I have never asked Puca for anything. His gifts came freely.

I understood his motivation. He wasn't really doing it for me. It was the same motivation that made me get out of bed and go face the bootlicking parasites in the throne room.

The good of Fae and humanity - duty.

Sitting on the stone throne swore me to this duty. I took it with my eyes wide open, never thinking I'd truly be alone. I was sure that Puca only accepted being named King for the same reason. He never believed Danu would leave his side.

I understood the sadness I'd glimpsed in his eyes before he quickly hid it away.

At least Janice is alive.

Danu wasn't, and there was no hope for Puca. Me...

Hope is for fools and children.

I couldn't run a realm on hope and cotton candy. This wasn't some surface daydream. The unicorns, here, would drown you and feed you to their young as a Kelpie. Pixies would chew you apart, and the only shifter I knew was Puca. It would be just my luck if a dragon decided to arrive and burn us all to death with an inadvertent cough.

The Fae in-waiting dressed my body and arranged my hair, then painted my face. It was all done in complete silence. The walls creaked to fill the void. The stone in the castle reflected my mood - solid and cold.

When I emerged from my rooms, the cold of my emotions had seeped into the entirety of the structure, leaving little doubt as to any reception in the throne room. I covered the well-worn path with quick, efficient steps, choosing to enter from the main door and not behind the stone seat.

Lavender announced my entrance, her lilac eyes glossing with unshed tears. My father, Cernunnos, stood on the opposite side of that wretched piece of rock. He exhibited no emotion, only a cold demeanor. His beautiful Fae features were as bland as baby food.

"Bow to our Queen!" Lavender ordered. She, too, carried the cold of my heart in the tip of her tongue. I barely had time to notice her violet hair, before my wings carried me to the throne, and I took my perch. She hummed for a moment to make a change to something I was wearing.

It saddened me that even Lavender was affected by Jacques' escape.

The line of Fae ran out the main door and into the courtyard like an unwound extension cord. It started out organized but quickly became a tangled mess.

The ass-kissers all carried smug smiles, holding their bodies in erect assurance. The black and white heads in the line were dotted with bits of color here and there. The first Fae came forward. It was an UnSeelie male, who was accompanied by his daughter. The male flipped his half cloak back over his shoulder.

I hummed for a protection bubble, and my wings beat down, raising me to my feet. The motion caused my father to lurch forward and pin the male to the stone floor. The girl screeched in shock.

"No, we aren't armed," the young Fae-ling mourned. Her pink hair was spiked and sharp around her face. She was still fresh from her chrysalis, the newness of Fae magic still clung to her aura, waking in a variety of colors. She was unaligned, her hair the same color as her chrysalis, with only the hint of white at the tip.

"The next time you enter the Queen's presence, you best leave the cloak at home," Cernunnos growled into the male's face.

The male blanched, causing him to look more like Dracula, than a Fae, with all his black hair and pointed features.

Cernunnos took to his full height which towered over the male and huffed. The male didn't bother to rise from the floor, only turned over so he could kneel for me.

"Forgive me, my Queen. I meant no offense. I came to ask clemency on my small family." He opened an arm to the Fae-ling, and she rushed to fill it.

I didn't reply.

Why should I?

He was going to tell me what he wanted, anyway. I glanced at Lavender.

"Don't waste the Queen's time. Get to the begging part," she remarked, and her normally sweet tone seemed to be gone. I never believed she would lose her eternal cheerfulness. However, today it seemed to be missing. I noted that as a conversation for later.

The male clasped his hands together, "Your Majesty, I am Thorda, a member of the Autumn court. Mod, our new Princess, has forced me from my humble abode, and I have nowhere to live in. I ask that you intervene on my behalf for a return of my lodgings and goods." He crossed his arm over his chest and his fingers too, before lowering his head. He, then, touched his fingers to his forehead.

His manners were nice. Too bad I was not going to stick my nose in Mod's business. She had work to do and I was sure he was part of it.

"Are you sworn to Jacques?" I asked point-blank.

"I was his vassal," he stammered as his body was coated in fear. The wakes around him quivered like water when something heavy hits the ground nearby.

"That is not what I asked." I snapped my fingers and his clothes fell to the floor, leaving him naked for the court. The Fae crowd twittered in amusement. "Search his things!" I ordered. Two guards moved from the walls and began picking through his clothes. The guards squatted and began running their fingers over the fabric, feeling for oddities and weapons. They came away with nothing, so they shrugged. I waved them back to their positions.

The male remained on his knees as if begging. The Fae-ling pulled a leather strip from around her neck. Hanging at the end of it was a ring with a red stone. "Here, take this as an offering." The female crouched next to her father, keeping her eyes trained on the floor. Her wakes waved with deception, and the tips of her hair lost more of the pink hue from her chrysalis.

One of the guards stepped forward to receive the gift. He grabbed it by the leather and brought it the few steps it took to reach me. The extended arm froze in front of me.

Lavender reached for the trinket, "Stop!" I shouted. The ring glinted in the Fae light and one of its facets shone in my eyes. For a moment, I was blinded by the ruby hue and its dazzle. The wakes coming from the stone hungered for me, and like magical hands, they grasped at me. The magic in the ring lured me in with its beauty. It begged me to possess it. Of its own volition, my hand tentatively reached out to attain this prize.

I held my breath for the beat of a robin's heart. The wakes in the room froze in time with the beat. I became that space between the beating of a heart, that moment between life and death. I became the place where you either exist or not.

The song tore from my throat. It was Fleetwood Mac with their Little Lies. It blasted through the throne room, slamming the doors closed, locking all inside. I closed my eyes to remember where I'd seen those wakes. My head whipped to Cernunnos. His head tilted down just a fraction.

"You would try to trick your Queen?" I screamed. The two UnSeelie liars' heads shot up. All subterfuge was lost as reality hit them full force.

"Tell me all your lies,

All your sweet little lies,

They are no longer a disguise."

I changed the main chorus.

The compulsion in my song forced them to begin speaking. "Jacques came to me and ordered me to give you the ring. He then changed his mind and demanded Pedal give it to you." The male stood in front of his Fae-ling, protecting her from me.

I whistled, and his body collided with the nearest Fae, and then the wall. I turned to the Fae-ling, "Did you swear an oath to Jacques? Did you choose?" I asked with my menacing voice. I bared my teeth, and my wings beat, pushing the hair back from her face. Her terror scented the room and her wakes. It was the perfect perfume for my feelings.

"No. He said that if I succeeded, he would take me into his court and train me," she stumbled over her words, then took to her feet. "I will face my punishment." She gulped at her bravado. Her wakes spoke of a barely held control.

I scanned the room. Someone there was watching for him. The ring still hung before me, so I glanced at my father. He took the offered ring, holding it by the leather thong. He held it up to his face, turning it in the light to inspect the stone. The crease between his brows deepened as his jaw grounded his teeth. He shot me a murderous stare and lowered the ring.

I turned back to the male standing before me. "Thorda, your punishment is death by pixies. Give him to the hedges!" Two guards dragged him away as I hummed a silencing spell over him to keep him from pulling a song from his hat.

"Do you wish to join your father in the hedges, Pedal?" I asked and cocked an eyebrow at her.

She faltered as her mouth opened and closed. Her hands fisted and then released. She swallowed and tilted her chin up to meet me. A second later, our eyes locked. "What would I have to do to save myself?" She asked with a stiff back.

"What were you made for?" I asked.

She must have been the last chrysalis the old Queen made. Pedal's clothes were still made of the leftover parts of her chrysalis.

"I'm a warrior. Father earned me." She was proud.

Who am I kidding? All Fae are proud.

"Swear your sword to my service, or go join the father you're so proud of," I remarked. "Then, return to Mod and help her with her quest. Tell all you meet what happens to Jacques' minions. Cross me and I'll fucking kill you in the worst way I can. Your father got off easy," I growled.

The Fae-ling didn't break a sweat as she swore her sword arm to my eternal service. After a while, the oaths all sounded the same, as the faces blurred, and the names blended.

Sending her to Mod was just icing on the UnSeelie cake. Turning the Autumn court against Jacques was strategic. I wanted him to have nowhere to go and no one to help him.

I surveyed the faces in the crowd, hoping the spies would give themselves away. Several hours later, my father laid a hand on my shoulder. I resisted for a moment, then allowed him to lead me away from the court. Lavender sent the brown nosers on their merry way and came to join us.

My ass plopped down in the special chair made for a Queen.

Because we can't just sit like normal people. Oh, no! We need a lower back to make way for our ridiculous wings.

I mentally grumbled.

"It's the same type of stone as the one in the king's staff," Cernunnos informed me.

I already knew that. Hearing him confirming it, just added to my woes.

Trouble comes in threes. This must be number three.

First, Janice left, then Jacques escaped, and now there was a new red stone.

The Queen killer.

"Jacques gave a similar stone to the second King after Oberon," he stated and a growl followed Puca's formal name.

Cernunnos would never forgive Puca for taking my mother away. Even if it did save my life, as well as hers. He believed that he could have saved her from the Queen.

I didn't have time for his petty delusions. However, it was laughable on a good day since my father still didn't understand the power of a Queen.

"What do you think he would get out of me wearing that thing?" I asked.

The wakes never stopped trying to reach me. The magic spell locked in that stone scared me. I could still feel the pull as it sucked me dry like a wet/dry vac, taking everything that made me Fae. The way the stone brightened with the added magic, made me sick to my stomach.

The dead bodies of the other contenders danced before my mind's eye. The blood that coated the floor of the throne room still haunted my dreams. All those girls were no more than a meal for the stone to chew up and spit out.

If there are two, there are more. And Danu help us, if they are all in Jacques' possession.

CHAPTER 7

MERCIA

The forest blurred as I moved through it with the speed of the wind. The sound of Nick following me broke the rushing of air over my ears. He sang for Jack several times to keep up. A smile cracked my face. The hunt was on, and even though the stakes were high, I was not alone in my quest. It was refreshing, as the last joint hunt I had was with Momma.

And that was so long ago.

It was fitting to have Nick at my side, since magic requires balance.

Overriding the thrill of the hunt or my newfound companion was a deep fear for the bowl.

How had Puca known there was an issue?

The ways of Oberon were not part of Fae's education. I studied the leaves on the trees as I passed them. The soil and moss were undisturbed. The rocky face of the sheared-off-hill loomed before me. Light pierced the darkness near the cave, and my insides tightened for the fight.

I dashed to out-flank them. Nick kept to my left, careful to provide me enough space to draw my bow. His guns were in his hands, and they waked with an unusual spell, one I didn't know but had seen before.

Sure shot.

The light in the forest surrounded the entrance to the cave, dancing with witches. Witch's light wasn't like Fae. It wasn't the same vibrant green. Witch's light burned red, the deep red of almost congealed blood with blue overtones. I didn't think they understood the meaning of that color or why it was so dark.

They were chanting, making me gulp.

This is bad.

The shadows from blocking the fire shifted with the chant. The shadows grew then shrunk.

My flittermouse chirped to me. He clung to the cliff, and I moved to his call. Nick moved with me. I flattened my back to the cliff and moved closer to the dancing light. I sang low.

"Sticks and stones may break my bones,
But witches' words shall never hurt me."

I side-eyed Nick, and he repeated the magic. His education was different from mine. My experience with witches went deeper than a sinkhole. I changed the wording and used the same song to morph the rocks and the cliff.

"Sticks and stones may break my bone,

But they shall never hurt me if they emerge from a wall."

The cliff face pushed the edges of rocks out at varying distances, creating stepping stones. I quickly took to the rocks. They maintained a level 20 feet off the ground. As I climbed, Nick followed.

The waking power of the cave grew, vibrating the rocks under my feet.

The mushroom inside never stopped growing and its magic warped the area from many yards away.

"Awe! Pixie shit!!!" I hissed.

Nick chuckled and replied, "This is a real problem. We should call Puca."

I scowled at him from over my shoulder. "We don't need Oberon to save us. That comes at a cost. I can handle this," I retorted under my breath.

"You sound like your mother. Arty would have accepted help," he replied as one of his feet joined one of mine on a rocky outcropping. He leaned in to whisper in my eyes. "Don't be foolish, Mercia."

I stiffened.

How dare he call me foolish! He lies to me, and now I'm foolish?

He extended his arm. Following the tip of his index finger, I saw the real problem. It wasn't Nick or his poor choice of words and deeds -we were outnumbered.

The fire was surrounded by a coven of eighteen witches. These weren't your run-of-the-mill, watered-down, generations-old changelings. These were quarter breeds or better. The power emanating from each one was distorted with layers of magic, both human and Fae. They were magical cakes with extra filling in the form of charms.

These witches were nothing like the Savannah hags. They were a powerful real deal.

"They're breeding for strength," Nick remarked.

The hair on my body rose. Watching them move with the fire, made me miss the blood ties. They were all generations of breeding. They carried bloodlines of the winter court, Deston's domain. I heaved a sigh.

At least they don't belong to Jacques.

Deston's changelings would be easier to get the upper hand. Jacques', on the other hand, we'd need Puca for them. I bit my lip to hold the whistle that lingered on my tongue.

"You still think we can handle this?" Nick inquired. He hummed over his equipment and various body parts, then moved to me.

"I don't need your help to gear up," I snarled.

Before I could turn away from him, he'd pushed my body against the cliff face. His feet were planted on the same rocks as mine. He was too close, yet I refused to meet his demanding stare. He had me trapped.

If I push him off, he'll fall right into the middle of the witch's circle.

He forced my head back. "We are a team. You're letting your emotions get in the way. I will not let you fail just because you are mad at me."

My heart double-stepped, and a fire raced over me. His wakes changed from a fight to lust. I wanted to welcome him, to take that emotion that was so freely offered. His moss-green eyes were lost in the darkness, and all I could make out were dark orbs, glinting in the moonlight.

"I don't need you to succeed," I growled and before I could stop myself, I licked my lips.

His mouth slammed into mine. He demanded entry, and I gave it to him. He dug deep into my soul and pulled out what I held hidden -I wanted him.

Then, it was over. His forehead pressed against mine. His hands cupped my face, and his thumbs moved over my cheeks. "I'm trying to prove you can trust me. Let me show you," he replied. I breathed in that scent that was so uniquely Nick's cologne and… I licked my lips once more. It was a beverage flavor from before the fall.

"Fine."

He released my face, and I pressed my mouth closed to stop a protest.

Love, play and a hunt don't mix.

I had to get control of myself.

Nick pulled the bow free of my grasp. He started to hum, and it grew into a deep chant. Magic waked over the bow, changing its normal state from the inertness of the human forest to something worthy of Fae.

The bow flashed the dark green of an old forest, and the surrounding wakes settled into that shade.

"Sure shot!" He handed the bow back to me. I blinked twice and tore my eyes away from the hastily made bow and its new spell.

"You learned it? How?" I asked.

He gave me a half-smile, "You think I just went looking for your shoes?" he shook his head and stepped up to the next set of rocks, giving me space to admire my new bow. "I'll teach you later."

We both refocused on the witches on the forest floor.

They had a circle made of salt. They believed that salt would save them.

That may work with humans, not Fae.

I whistled like the wind, coaxing the grass and moss to absorb the salt, breaking the circle. At my side, Nick called to the wind to blow the salt away, making the line thin.

The sound of their chants grew to a new and frenzied level. Three of the witches weren't inside the circle and added fresh salt to the line.

I flared my nostrils in irritation.

"Rain, rain, come my way,

Come and wash my enemies away."

I left off the rest of the song. I didn't need thunder to light my way or that of my enemy. The sky rumbled nonetheless, and the moon's light disappeared behind heavy clouds.

The sky shivered with its heavy-weight. A moment later, the sky opened to release its burden. Fat drops of water hit the forest's canopy, slipping past the leaves to the ground.

I sang again,

"Rain, rain come my way,

Come and wash my enemies away."

The rain intensified from a downpour to a monsoon. The salt washed away with the growing flood.

Nick hummed to the roots in the cliff, and they reformed into handles. I gripped the nearest root to keep from slipping off the rocks. My feet remained planted firmly on the outcropping.

The women in the circle never stopped singing. Instead, their voices grew to a screeching. The music was lost, leaving only the vibrations to twist the magic.

There was nothing for it. I had to stop them. The magic wakes surrounding the cave provided a shield to keep intruders out. It was weakening.

In a few minutes, the shield will be gone.

"Lighting, thunder come my way,

And burn a path, to light my way."

I sang for the electricity. With as much water as it was on the ground, it could kill a few of them.

The sky crackled with new power. I drew out the last two words, and Nick's tenor joined my voice. His hand found mine, and we joined our magical call. The thunder rolled right over our heads, a moment before the lightning crashed into the ground, illuminating the forest floor.

Three witches keened in pain and slumped to the ground. The hair of the three outside the circle were on fire.

I glanced over to Nick, who nodded. Then we both leaped down to the forest floor. I knocked an arrow, and loosed the first round. I hit a witch and lodged in her heart. She fell dead on the spot. I quickly pulled two more in succession. A wicked sense of joy flowed over me. The thrill of the hunt coursed through my veins anew. Both witches fell. Nick's gun cut the forest down, never hitting a mark.

The witches in the circle had a bubble of protection, and the projectiles bounced off. A piece of iron shot past me and embedded it in the tree near me. The waking of the iron burned that side of my face.

"They have iron!" I shouted at Nick.

"Noted," he hollered back.

Turning away from the circle, I dashed for the cave.

If I can grab the bowl, Nick can open a portal, and we can be done with this.

The chanting reached a crescendo, and the blast of magic joined the momentum of my movements, slamming me into the rocky cliff. My eyes rolled around in my head for a moment. Roots started to grow over me, as a woman's voice cut through the malaise. She sang a lullaby, making my eyes grow heavy, but the intended sleep never overwhelmed me.

My limbs eased their tension, sleeping like the spell the witch sang. My mouth refused to answer my brain's demands. The rain from my storm poured down the side of the cliff, soaking me to the bone and clogging my mouth.

I couldn't free myself. I was stuck there.

For now.

I closed my eyes to keep the water out and fool my tricky prey.

"Mon petite, she's a pretty one," one witch remarked.

"Leave her! She won't be able to break free of the forest," an old woman ordered.

"What about this hot piece of warlock flesh?" A younger woman asked and giggled.

"We need better breeding stock," the old woman replied.

The sound of footsteps retreating through the underbrush informed me of my predicament. So, I hummed the roots away and fell at the base of the cliff.

The only light left came from my birth cave and the mushroom within. The orange light glowed through the cracks in the cliff for anyone to see. The light from the mushroom was fading.

I clawed my way to the crevasse, dragging my sleeping legs behind me.

My forest friends all chirped in greeting and mourned the loss of their daylight protection. The base of the mushroom had been hacked away, and the mushroom was shriveling. The base wilted away as only the hollow where the bowl was once hidden remained. The flange my chrysalis once clung to shrunk, and for the first time since Momma died, I really cried.

Momma and everything about her were finally gone. Only I remained. A rage tore through me.

How dare they steal my mother's magic and my birthright?

The bowl belonged to me and mine, not to some mangy witches living in a swamp.

Why, why did Puca have to be right?

Puca was going to kill me.

I whispered my thanks to the flittermouse and freed them from their obligation to me and Momma. They refused and offered to help me find the bowl. Rather than deny their help, I pressed my lips closed on the human *thank you* that lurked there. Flittermice revered Fae and all its ways. They would scoff at such a reply.

I called on the green Fae fire and burned what was left of Momma's mushroom. I couldn't risk any more mutts finding the leftover magic and using it.

I ducked outside and scanned the area for Nick. The forest floor was a disaster. Between the water and the fire, there wasn't much left. A bundle of smoking logs smoldered in the clearing. Broken branches and lost leaves lay scattered in the area, making the trees groan from the loss of energy.

I hummed the song of renewal, helping the trees replace what was taken from them. The witches cut down a tree to light their circle fire. They could have gathered more than enough from the forest floor, but they chose the easy path. There was no need for this kind of theft.

Nature always provides.

The bodies of the witches I'd killed were gone. Also, there was no sign of Nick. I hummed a tracker spell, and thirteen witch trails appeared all around Nick's green one.

They left together.

My heartbeat stopped and my mouth dried, remembering what the old woman said about breeding stock. *Nick!*

CHAPTER 8

SARAH

Part of me wanted to crush this stone like I had the other. Doing so wouldn't answer all the questions, I had rolling around in my head.

How did he make it? What type of stone is it? Are there more? Can I use it as a weapon?

Even though it was red, it wasn't a ruby. The color was earthy and glowing. It was more of the burning ember of a fire than the blazing red of a sunset. Its magical wakes matched the color of the stone. It reached for me in different ways, sometimes resembling sharp claws, other times a warm blanket. It didn't matter how the magic wanted me. My skin crawled with ants just looking at it.

"What is it made of?" I looked from Cernunnos to Lavender.

My father glanced at Lavender, "Get the record keeper. Tell him to bring the Book of Jillian."

Lavender blanched and stumbled into the hallway. Her reaction confused me. Jillian was long dead, and other than the story of her and Jacques, nothing explained why a book about her would matter.

"Perhaps we should call Oberon," I remarked.

Cernunnos slicked his black hair back from his forehead. "That is your choice. There is a price for his help. All know this. You of all people can't afford to owe him." His brows pulled down, giving his normally handsome face a dark turn, reminding me of how we first met. The sight of him covered in the leaves of wyld came and went with a flash.

"Sharing information is not the same as asking a favor." The word games made me crazy. The semantics of it all worked my patience over faster than a quicksilver blade.

My father paced to the window that looked down on Tatiana's garden. That Queen had a knack for growing plants - poisonous plants, the kind that kill in the most horrid ways. You could die taking a morning stroll if you didn't keep to the path.

Tatiana liked to toss her victims out this window and watch them as they met their fate. I shivered. I didn't want to be known for my ability to kill.

Yet, every corner I go around, leads me to the next threat that must be eliminated.

Fear wasn't the only way to rule. It was just the Fae way. I closed my eyes to the harshness of my world. The deep breath I pulled into my lungs was to cleanse my mind. It didn't work, and neither did the counting to five, ten, or fifteen. I could count to kingdom come and it wouldn't lessen the load.

I needed to find my way out of this maze of death and power struggles that I was in. However, no path presented itself to me. I felt like I never left the maze in Jacques' garden. It was like I was still wandering around, searching for the way out that wasn't there.

The door to my office opened, pushing a scant amount of air towards me. I opened my eyes to find a strange-looking creature. It was heavily robbed and hunched over. White hair trailed down to the floor from under the large drooping hood. Its long and thin spider leg like fingers were clutched onto an old weathered tome.

Lavender flourished her arm to indicate the being now standing before me, "The record keeper." She provided no sexual indication nor name, as if the title alone was all that was necessary.

Ugh!

Everything about it reminded me of the Dark Crystal movie. I was looking for the puppet strings, but none arrived.

The Record Keeper bowed with a grace I hadn't expected and laid the tome on my desk. Having never seen a book older than 50 years or so, I wasn't sure what to expect. The Fae and their library were secretive to begin with.

Each prince had an archive of their own and maintained it viciously. The emissaries I sent to Jacques' domain weren't able to gain access to his library, and Deston's was already eaten by the magic before they got there.

Nick told me there was nothing of true value in Jacques' private rooms.

Janice.

Just the thought of him stopped my train of thought and turned the air I breathed into poison. All I could do was choke on the emotions I couldn't display.

Janice searched Deston's rooms and came back with nothing.

The Record Keeper opened the book and flipped through pages so fast I couldn't get a grip on anything. The creature finally settled two-thirds of the way in on an elaborate picture of the king's staff.

Only then did it speak, "The walls recorded the presentation of the King's staff. It was a gift from Jacques to our newly named King after Oberon was released from service. King Verdedon accepted it with grace. The Queen stewed over Jacques' lack of gift for her." The voice was liquid oil, slithering in your inner ear. It left behind an insatiable itch like warm wax after wearing earbuds.

Even after having heard the being speak, I could tell no more about it. The wakes of magic coming from the creature spoke of age and wisdom, but most of all, they spoke of danger.

The creature said the walls recorded.

They listen.

The walls had always shown me kindness. However, before that, I never saw them for what they were - spies. Rather than rear back from this new revelation it was time to use it.

"Who else has been through the records since I took the throne?" I asked.

"Finian, then Jacques," the creature replied. Its hand, covered in the rich yellow marking of Fae, reached for the book as if to take it, and I laid my hand over the tome.

"I sealed the library. How is it they gained access?" I pulled the old book towards me and began leafing through the pages.

"The King has always been granted access along with a guest," was the oily reply.

I ground my teeth down on a retort. "What did the walls record about that trip?" I hissed.

"Jacques dug into the stone well and Danu's private journals. He did not take anything, but he labored over one in particular." The creature's robes rose and fell as it breathed, being the only sign of life.

I pushed the Fae into the floor with the snap of my fingers and the wave of a hand. "You will let none into the library without my presence. Swear it!" no sound came. "Now!" I shouted.

"I swear it." For a moment, the voice had the tilt of a female before it quickly slipped away.

"Bring me Danu's journals." I waved the creature out and Cernunnos escorted the Fae back to its domain.

I glanced at the walls and sang.

"I always feel like somebody's watching me."

The song froze the walls, turning the room cold and lifeless.

"I need you to read those journals. Whatever that ring is, it's bigger than just one or two stones. If Jacques was researching it, he didn't even know what it was," I whispered and glanced out the window.

"My lady, stories of the stone well or circle are as old as Fae and they are many. How will I know when I've found what we need?" Lavender clasped my hand in hers. Fear bled from her. She never wanted any of this life at court. She was content helping her brother run his principality.

"I trust you," was all I could say.

There was no need to say more. Her cheeks colored with embarrassment. She quickly wrapped me in her arms and whispered, "I won't let you down."

"You never have."

She let go to follow her brother and the Record Keeper. Lavender had a talent I was not sure she understood. Most Fae couldn't see what I could - the strands of magic that wove together to create each and every Fae. It really was like making a cake or mixing spices. Lavender had the latent talent of patterns. She could pick them out, whether it was with clothes and colors or behavior and motive.

The talent of pattern finding was as simple as the spiral of a nautilus shell and as complex as the internal structure.

To be pretty requires more to please the eye than color. It requires balance.

Lavender would find it whatever it was. She had the ability to find the thing that was out of balance. I was banking on it.

The tome before me smelled of age, dust, and of that something that old vellum takes on after several hundred years.

Or in this case, thousands?

I didn't know. The only thing I knew was that the book looked fucking old.

The King's staff leaped from the page. It was an illumination, or so I thought. The art style reminded me of an old storybook I found in the school library called Canterbury Tales. All the pictures were edged in a reflective gold material. At the time, the librarian told me it wasn't gold but meant to resemble it. Some of the original copies of that book had the same pictures.

I loved the stories and the funny circles on the heads of the friars.

A Fae illumination actually glowed. The gold shimmered with magic. Every color carried that day-glow light from the Hallowed Hills.

I turned the page to read the story, but there were only more pictures. Turning to another page, I came face to face with yet more drawings, until I finally reached the last page.

George was holding the King's staff over Jillian. A red light connected Jillian's heart to the beating heart of the red stone. The longer I stared at the page, the older Jillian became. Her white hair's gloss faded as did her Fae markings. The pink bow of her lips shrunk, and the teeth in her mouth disappeared. The hand she held in the air as if to protect herself from the magic of the staff grew too heavy and dropped. Her body sagged against the floor, and her head laid down until she was nothing more than a dry bag of bones lying on the throne room floor.

Her corpse looked as dry as my mouth felt. My heart squeezed with every beat, turning over in my chest. I could feel the phantom stone sucking my magic away. The waking world ceased to move, and all I saw was life as a human.

Jillian didn't have the life of a human to fall back on, and the stone sucked her dry of everything.

A single tear traced its way down my cheek.

Jacques did this to her and every Queen after her. But why?

I flipped back to the beginning of the book to find a battlefield. Puca sat on a horse next to the most exquisite woman I'd ever seen—Danu. Her wings were golden, as were her light Fae markings. It was her green eyes that arrested me. Her posture on the white stead was that of a Queen and her crown as golden as she was. She resembled my mother a bit.

Except the eyes.

Jillian and Jacques were on the opposite side of the battlefield, intentions were announced, and the battle began.

The book didn't need words. Every page played like a movie, leading you from one important moment to the next. At the end of the battle, Danu whispered something to Puca, and he left. She then handed a stone bowl to another Fae.

I was shocked. Puca loved her, yet he left when she needed him most. Tears threatened to break free from my eyes and fall. I wasn't crying for Danu, but me.

I am crying for me.

Janice left. Just like Puca.

I guess Fae men are all the same. They get while the gettin' is good. Fuckers!

CHAPTER 9

MERCIA

The hunter's trail led me out of the forest and into marshland. My flittermouse friends traveled with me. Their concern over the loss of the stone bowl was interesting.

Maybe, Momma told them about it?

That was stupid thinking, since Momma wasn't a talker, but a doer. The safety of both Fae and humanity relied on keeping the stone bowl safe. Not that I understood why. Puca, like Momma, only told you what you needed to know.

And nothing more.

Right now, I felt like I really needed to know what the fuck that bowl was for!!!

Inside, I was screaming.

If I'd have moved faster?

Puca asked me to leave sooner, and I didn't listen. What if I'd listened to Nick and whistled for Puca?

Ugh! Danu, take me!

I leaped from dry place to dry place, in an attempt to keep my feet in good condition. That was until I came to a rickety wooden landing covered in scuff marks.

A boat, they'd taken a boat.

The trees sticking out of the water offered no free branches for me to weave a vessel from, making my forest friends chirp their urgings. They couldn't understand why I wasn't moving forward.

"I don't have a pigeon-crapping boat!" I yelled. The sound bounced off the trees at my back and created ripples on the water. Both hands gripped either side of my head as I screamed out my frustration. An old flittermouse landed on my shoulder and bit himself, offering his blood to make a circle.

Tears I knew I shouldn't shed pooled in my eyes, and a long-forgotten love for my forest friends bloomed inside me.

"No, you can't bleed for me. It doesn't work that way. Your blood won't work," I muttered over the lump in my throat.

His sacrifice was all for me. He remembered me from when I was young. They didn't know Nick, yet they were willing to die to help me. All at once, that feeling of being alone in the world evaporated.

Momma has left me a silent nighttime army.

I sang to heal my little friend, grateful I could. I pulled one of my finger daggers from my bodice. "I'm coming," I called to my friends as they swooped over the dank water.

I sliced the inside of my off arm enough to bleed, not enough to damage, dripping it in a circle, and quickly wrapping it up. The blast of magic as the mushrooms grew together and formed my fairy circle was a shock.

Inside the round, the air spoke of Fae and the many delights of the hallowed hills. Its call washed over me like the warm bath I would need to take when this hunt was over. The space around the small round shivered with magical distortion.

Momma told me to never bleed a round. To avoid travel by the skies. That humans knew our tricks and would shoot us down.

I drug my glistening eyes away from the round and its magical whispered promises of Fae perfection. I stared out across the water at the hunter's trail. Nick's green line shone bright against the darkness. My heartbeat skipped. This was a step I had to take.

Not just to get Nick, but Ron too.

I could count at least fifteen reasons to use the round and only one not to.

Momma, I've got to do this. I know you would understand if it was daddy.

I gulped and stepped into the distorted air of the round, and the whispered song of Fae. I sang a song of flying and the round lifted into the air, tearing free of the landing. There was no doubt a Fae had been there and left by air.

I glanced back to survey the area, and my eyes caught a lone mushroom on the landing. It glowed a dark hunter's green. It couldn't be Nick's as his were the color of moss. It was definitely mine.

At least now I know what color mushrooms I make.

I threw fairy fire on it and left the dock to burn. There was no way I would leave anything useful behind for those witchy bitches.

The flittermice swooped around my head, and I sang us forward over the water. If all we needed to do was follow the marsh and their trail, this would be over easily. Instead, they ran their boat up onto a patch of dry land that abutted an old road.

The plants grew right up to edges and all around. The only telltale sign was in fact, a road full of rusted-out cars and trucks from the fall. Some colors still peeked through the corrosion and vines, while others were just the earthy reds of time and decay. It was nothing I hadn't seen before. The transportation from before the fall all looked the same. These were only different in one way - there were so many of them, and they were all lined up. Every car stuffed together bumper to bumper, without an inch to spare. The only space was the center line between them.

The cement was still black with cracked chunks of faded yellow. My Fae sight made it easy to pick out the line that was once painted there.

Rather than chance the witches leaving traps and tricks, I kept to my round and floated over the magic trail.

A scent I was not familiar with reached me. I crinkled my nose. It was rotting trash, the kind humans leave, old water, food bits, or human waste.

Things nature doesn't like, and a Fae wouldn't leave. Well, things I wouldn't leave.

The trash prompted my training, and I pulled the don't look here song out for my protection. If I could glamor, I could sneak right in and steal Nick away. It would be no more than taking a cookie from a table.

But that gamble was a long one. If they were indeed breeding for Fae traits, then I might not fool them all.

And then what?

I shook my head. I'd work that out when I got there. How long would it take them to figure out Nick wasn't just a warlock? And what kind of spells would they use on him to get him to comply with their breeding plans?

Something told me Nick wouldn't be forced into anything. Tricked maybe, but not forced.

Is Nick as valuable as the bowl?

He said that humans with access to someone like us would be dangerous. I'd seen what the Govs would do first hand.

The meaty part of my palm rubbed at my hip where that human had cut me open to drill my bone marrow. The phantom scars and pain still haunted me. The reality of good versus evil would never be far from my mind. Being used for sex and babies isn't as bad as being cut up for parts. But it wasn't much better either.

One kills you quickly. The other in bits and pieces as they rape your body and soul.

I'd seen what happens to women who are passed around against their will. I didn't want that for Nick or Ron.

The wind kicked up, and the heat from my shame was wicked away. I hadn't thought about Ron in weeks. I was too focused on myself and my problems.

The Govs have Ron, Witches have Nick and I got bats. Hundreds of them.

Every tool was a weapon. Whistling into the wind, I called a few flittermice to me. "Scout ahead. I need intel on where we're going."

The older bat swooped twice as if gathering his squad and flew on in the direction of the road while others took to the East and West sides, covering the bayou and marsh-covered land.

I moved as fast as I dared with the cover of darkness, keeping close to the trees lining the road. A young flittermouse landed on my shoulder. He was fresh from the nest and needed a respite.

His little heartbeat a staccato rhythm against my shoulder. The excitement of the hunt was chirped in my ear. I once sounded like him.

Now, I am the old hand.

It was a new responsibility for me. One I was not sure I wanted. Teaching the next generation wasn't part of my plan. However, friendship comes at a cost, and this was it. The flittermice had taught me the ways of the forest along with momma.

My old friend returned, winging his way back and forth, sharing the story of the road. The line of cars ended not far ahead. That was only because the road collapsed into the water. The forest fell away from the road and rose up into the air. I rose with it.

The edge reminded me of the jump-off of the bridge back in my old city. Cement bits crumbled away from the broken edge. Rebar stuck out at all angles, covered in rust and gleaming with particles of iron.

I moved my round further away to keep the waking magic of iron from burning my skin or leaking power away from me.

That is the last thing I need.

Off in the distance, parts of the old road peeked out of the water for miles. Like arteries, to the heart of the Mississippi Delta, the water and roads, all lead to one place — New Orleans. The dim glow of artificial light rose up from the water.

For once, I wished Nick was right. I wanted to believe that the city truly was under water and the threat wasn't true. I wanted to believe that Momma had exaggerated the power of the witches there.

Why couldn't her experience from before the fall be just that?

Floating boards gathered at the base of a cement piling. I hummed it onto a portion of the raised roadway and lowered my round. The floating lumber was rotten. Although, with a bit of magic with the addition of my round, I would be the proud owner of a flat-bottom bayou boat.

I sang 'row, row, row your boat' and waited for the magic to do its work. My feet tiptoed on to my new mode of transport. I took a seat. A few of the bats joined me for the sit-down and remarked how the underside of some of the old highways would make a suitable resting place come daylight.

I smirked at how simple a solution that was for them, then scanned the sky for the telltale signs of dawn. It wasn't far off, and I was surrounded by water. There wasn't going to be much time to reach the city and find safety for the coming of the day.

I flared my nostrils and sang for Jack to give me speed, then began rowing for my life.

CHAPTER 10

SARAH

I slammed the book shut and took to my rooms. When that wasn't enough to calm me, I walked the gardens. Every Queen designed a garden. Some were gorgeous, others a terror. I liked the water garden best as the tinkling of water falling from all the fountains drowned out the roaring in my ears.

I wanted to get out of this shitty dress and throw on a pair of jeans and a t-shirt, grab my gun and find Janice myself.

I'll look desperate, it's true, but at least I'll be doing something.

All this standing around, waiting for Mod or Lavender to bring me something was killing me.

I kicked the nearest rock. It ricocheted off the side of one of the many fountains and flew back, hitting me in the ankle.

"Cocksucker!" I rubbed the bone. There was a small cut where the raw edge of the rock nicked me. Rather than cause more damage, I sat on the lip of a fountain. My wings trailed into the water at my back and I wilted.

I quickly surveyed the garden before allowing myself one tear. It slipped down my cheek and ran into my cleavage. One would normally be followed by two, before turning into a waterfall.

That isn't going to happen.

Instead, bile burned in my belly, so I stood up with a rush.

"I'm through with this crap. No more sitting around. I'm not waiting for shit to happen." With a down beat of my wings, I was at the door to the castle. My feet barely touched the stone floor before I was in my room.

I snapped my fingers and all my clothes lay on the ground in pieces. I whirled my hands in the air and whistled. The cotton flowers on the floor turned into a T-shirt. I called all the leather in the room to me, and encased my body.

Puca would be proud.

The door to my wardrobe slammed open and I pulled Silver, my sword, out and strapped it around my waist. The shoulder strap for my Khan 380 handgun came next. I slid the gun into position and pulled my jacket on. My wings found their way through the accommodating holes. I felt normal for the first time since I sat on that stupid rock.

Jacques was counting on me to be sitting on my ass like all the other Queens, that I would wait for him to make his move and send others to do my bidding.

Well, that ain't gonna happen.

I wouldn't have taken the stone throne, if I did what was expected.

Winners don't sit on their ass. They make a play for what they want.

This was a *winner takes it all kind* of game, and I was going to play.

I stormed down the hallway to the throne room and banged the Queen's door open. The crowd fell down in the various curtsies, and bowed the pretend homage they paid to their sovereign.

"Rise!" I ordered. I glanced around, taking in the shocked faces. The vibration of song started in my belly where the vitriol lived, and I laced my magic with the burn. After that, I wove a heavy dose of compulsion into my words,

"Tell me your secrets, tell me your lies."

The song was more of a whisper of notes. I watched the magic wakes work their way around the room.

All Fae had secrets. I didn't want them all. We didn't have the time, and frankly, I didn't give two or three thousand fucks. I only wanted the secrets about Jacques, that silver-eyed assclown. He made me look like a fool. He was playing the long game, while I rested on my laurels.

Nothing made me madder than a hatter than being out-maneuvered. I snorted at the vision that leaped through my mind of Puca in a dapper waistcoat with a watch.

Compulsion works like a swat team using crowd control on a mob. First, it explodes. In this case, I was the point of impact. Then, it moves out from there as teargas. It fills the room, and surrounds the occupants, causing many to fall where they stand. Next, are the convulsions. Fae didn't like to give up their secrets, so they fought, and I was afraid it hurt a tinny, tiny, little bit.

Who am I kidding?

It hurts like hell. I was not sorry. If you had so many secrets, it was going to kill you to hold them in. well maybe you should die.

I mean, that many secrets has got to weigh a ton.

After most of the convulsions are over, comes the foaming at the mouth.

It's gross.

In Fae, the foam came in different colors and the brown one was just nasty.

Now, some pass out at this phase.

Those are the ones that have nothing for me.

Anyone still awake had a goodie or two, just for me.

I stood next to the stone throne with my arms crossed, and waited for the foam to settle. I expected one to still be awake. not four.

Jacques had been at this longer than I had. So, who knows how many were really out there? I stepped over the still bodies, doing my best to make sure I didn't get any of that nasty puke on my shoes until I reached my first contender.

He was smallish with owl-shaped eyes. They stared up at me, pleading to set him free of his misery. My toe nudged his shoulder urging him to lay on his back. In his weakened state, he complied. The light blue foam edged his mouth and bubbled down his neck. His lips resembled the color of someone suffocating to death. That wasn't his problem. No, his problem was much worse.

I squatted next to him and pulled my weapon from its holster. I gazed at the safety, then at the Fae male. "You know something. This is your one chance. Don't waste your life for Jacques. He would just as quickly give you to a kelpie to save himself." I nudged his chin with the barrel of the gun to urge him along.

"My Queen-"

"Don't bother with the '*my Queen*' bullshit. If I was your Queen, you wouldn't be helping Jacky-boy. Get to the point." A rumble fluttered in my belly.

"Jacques," he swallowed and closed his eyes. "He and Finian are together," he finished.

The trigger squeezed so easily. I hardly realized I'd pulled it. I moved my finger to the side of the barrel so I wouldn't do it again. The Fae lay there with a giant gaping hole between his eyes. His blue blood spread out on the floor from the exit wound on the back of his head.

I should have waited.

Maybe he had more to say?

"Who's next." I asked the room, No one raised their hand. Not that I thought they would. My eyes trailed over the form of Cernunnos standing in the doorway.

"Sarinha, would you like me to clean up the mess?" My father asked.

"Nope, no reason. I'm not done," I replied and stepped over a few bodies to get to my next victim. This male was bigger. He had the build of a warrior, the male version of Mod. He lay flat on his back, arms flung wide. The pink foam was still clogging his mouth. I sang for water and it pooled in my hand, then I dumped it in his face.

The adrenaline from the first kill jetted through my veins, jacking me up. "Wakey, wakey, eggs and bacy," I sang, forcing his eyes wide open.

He stared at me with pure abject terror. I straddled his chest, locking his arms to his sides, and leaned forward, then whispered, "Tell me your secrets."

"Jacques wants you dead, so he can rule," the male sputtered.

My eyes almost rolled out of my head. I raised my gun.

"Wait! Don't kill me! He went to the library looking for the stone well of Danu. He said that with it and the bucket, he could do something. I don't know what, but it's something to do with Danu and the making of Fae." He waked with the truth of his words. Yet, that wasn't going to save him. I didn't leave threats on the board. I cleared them.

The blast from the barrel only shocked my father, not me. I moved to the next bubbling mouth.

"Perhaps we could torture them a little longer and get more information before killing them." Cernunnos was a good one to talk. He'd been born a hunter, a killer.

I cocked an eyebrow at him. "I'm big mad. So, don't get in my way, Father," I growled with extra emphasis on the word *father*. Why he thought he could question anything was beyond me.

I smiled down at the next doucheberg in the room and placed my foot on her neck. A little voice in my head said it was wrong. But the devil on my shoulder pointed out Orwell's boot on the face was for mankind, not Fae. So the momentary guilt evaporated with my white-hot rage.

"Talk and don't jerk me off! I'm so not in the mood."

The female gurgled and swallowed the yucky brown foam. My nose curled in disgust.

"Nasty," I murmured.

"Finian took Janice." Her eyes never wavered.

My head whipped around to my father, "Take her to an iron room and work her over!" I ordered.

I, then, leaped to the last ballsack in the room. His eyes rolled around in his head. He was curled in a ball, rocking just a bit.

"Spill it!" I didn't bother to threaten him. He could already see the writing on the walls. The walls were as blue as the Fae blood that I'd just painted them with.

"Jacques is gathering his forces," he moaned.

I kicked him in the kidney, "Where?" I put my gun away and pulled Silver from her sheath with a metallic ring.

The aura of the male turned yellow and sour with his cowardice. "He's gathering weapons in the battle forest with the purple mushrooms."

"That forest is gone. I took it down myself." The sword danced across his skin.

The design was a simple V. I found it funny. Though, I was sure that I was the only one who got the joke. The word *Vicissitude* came to mind, an unforeseen change in one's circumstance.

I was sure that the dead Fae on the floor would have thought so if they could still think.

The blue blood oozed from the shallow cuts and pooled on his sternum before tracing its way down either side of his neck. A thrill raced through me with his blood loss. For once, I was enjoying the kill.

Is this what Cernunnos meant when he speaks of 'the thrill of the hunt?'

Because I was indeed hunting - I was hunting for information. I shook that away. Arty wouldn't let me lose myself over this, and Janice would keep me grounded.

I huffed air out through my nose.

They aren't here. It's just me.

"Try again," I sang.

"He wants you to meet him there so he can kill you. He says he has something that will end this."

I didn't wait for more. I sliced his head from his shoulders, then looked back at the people lying on the floor.

Three cadavers and a bunch of sleeping subjects.

These were the first three people I killed on purpose. I wanted to kill them. And I would do it all over again.

I turned to Cernunnos, "Now, you can clean up the mess if you want. Or you can leave it as a warning to the next guy who wants to spy for Jacques. I don't care."

I sang to wake up the populous lying on the floor.

"This is what happens when you side against me." I waved my hands at the bodies on the floor, "I… Eliminate… You!" I announced to the blurry-eyed sycophants as they sat up and wiped their faces clean of the foam.

CHAPTER 11

MERCIA

My hunter's cloak settled over my glamor, hiding not only myself, but the makeshift boat I'd scrambled together. I stopped rowing, only to make the glamor of driftwood work. Dipping oars would be a dead giveaway, or so I thought.

The bayou was vast, and the highway from before the fall resembled a snake in the water, with different portions dipping in and out. It made it hard to gauge how long the road really was. Most of the city appeared to be under water. However, there were some sections of dry land, but they were dry only by the hand of magic.

At the center of the dry spot, amongst all that water there were graveyards. The bodies wouldn't stay underground long without magic to push the water back. Whatever was in the ground was pushing the water back.

Not a spell or a song.

My forest friends didn't like this kind of magic. The old ones claimed it broke the cycle of the forest. One said it stole food.

A smile stole across my face. I imagined that the flittermouse was thinking of all the food they eat that starts its life in water. Insects of many varieties place larvae in water. Removing stagnant water would stop that cycle of life.

"This is not right. The dead shouldn't mettle in the world of the living," I muttered under my breath.

Bats understood how nature works. Anything that broke that cycle was their enemy. A few of them flew off to the North.

"Where are they going?" I asked my cauldron of bats. The old one chirped, 'For the colony. This must be stopped.'

I came here to rescue Nick and retrieve the bowl. However, it looked like I started a war. Staring out across the murky water, I wondered how many other animals would come to my aid.

But why would they do my bidding?

I emerged from the chrysalis as a hunter.

Wouldn't that make all prey?

I had two sides and like a coin, I could flip so easily.

I was not like most changelings. Most were born in the human way. I was born both human and Fae. My Fae side was all hunter, hungry for the kill, ready for the fight. However, my human side was weak. It forced tears from my eyes and emotions I didn't want. It kept me from my Fae brethren.

Humans coddle and coax their young while Fae break them with the fire of song to reforge them into something stronger.

I couldn't see my traits. I only knew what I felt and experienced.

This newfound ability to sway life on the surface scared me. Backing away from what I was, was not how I operated. It was a new challenge, something to conquer and hone. It was a weapon. Human or Fae, it shouldn't matter.

I swore to protect both for their own good.

The city of New Orleans no longer occupied the dry land. Humanity had spent almost two hundred years holding back water using various methods. Over time, a dike was the trusted tool. That kind of trust was gone.

Now, New Orleans, was a city lived from the second story up. Every ground floor of a building was under water. All those streets where humans celebrated Fat Tuesday were gone. The only floats going down Bourbon street were flat-bottomed boats pushed by long poles. The roof of houses dotted the watery landscape as I floated into the heart of this horrible place.

I decided to reveal my little boat, but not before rubbing mud over my arms and face to hide my Fae marking. I glamored as much as I dared. Any witch with too much Fae blood might see the song obscuring my true self. I tucked my shadowy hunter's cloak back into the world of unsung magic and hummed a lost pole from the bottom of the bayou to push my boat along.

The wood was slick with muck from lying in the slit. Old dead Spanish moss clung to the knots of the wood. Even though the pole was as crooked as a dog's leg, it was enough to push me along. Funny enough, there were no dogs here. I didn't expect any. Fae used dogs as pets like my flittermice to spy.

I floated past more rotting roofs and two-story homes with black vacant windows, waiting to sink into the water and join their neighbors. Underneath all the bramble and decaying homes in the water, I could feel IT.

Iron defined New Orleans and kept the Fae away from the moment it was built. Paris was built the same way, along with Savannah.

Iron.

It was woven into the very fabric of this city. Witches, half-Fae or less, didn't feel it. The effects were a mild aversion and nothing more.

Yet, for someone like me, it could be certain death. Momma told me Fae only encountered iron on the surface because Queen Jillian hunted iron in the Hallowed Hills and had it all removed.

I had a close encounter with iron the likes of which I never wanted to relive. Nick saved me. My heart fluttered at the memory of him singing my injuries away. His tenor was so clear, and the love he spoke of cutting me to the quick even now. The slow, steady movement of thrusting my pole into the water and pushing my boat along stopped. I choked back a cry that hung in my throat.

I didn't have time to cry over Nick and whatever feelings I had about him. I closed my eyes, swallowed the lump in my throat, and slapped each side of my face. When I opened my eyes again, the fog of worry was gone, leaving only the clear-sightedness of a killer on the hunt. The thrill raced through me, my blood gaining speed with all the ways I would need to infiltrate this coven and make away with my prey.

The rhyming of my words invigorated me further. I quickly thrust the pole in to pick up my pace.

A fog lingered in the air. It smelled of bayou and rotting plants. Bits of trash floated in the water. As I passed old buildings, sticking out of the water, my boat pushed the water and trash against the structure. The first of many docks formed out of the fog. Sitting on the edge, was a black cat with yellow eyes.

I gave it a cursory glance, and one of the flittermice offered to watch the cat. It referred to the feline as a *nature traitor*.

The term was interesting.

Fae bend nature to their will all the time, and in any way they deem appropriate.

For some reason, the flittermice didn't like cats amongst witches. I had never bent nature in a destructive manner. It wasn't the hunters' way.

We work with the landscape so our passing goes unnoticed.

Making grand gestures in an unnatural way went against the hunters' code.

We are only here to stalk and kill our prey, then slip away, not change the world.

I shook my head at the flittermice and their new term. I wondered how many Fae would fall under that name? What would the bats do if they discovered those infractions? It was neither here nor there. The Fae were all locked in the Hallowed Hills, never to return to the surface. Other than Puca, Nick, and myself, all that remained were the watered-down children of the changeling, witches, and warlocks.

The various docks were interconnected like Venice. The city wasn't defined by canals. Instead, the raised walkways connected the buildings and dry land, creating a world surrounded by water. On every dock was a cat with some black most orange calico.

The orange calico cats were all girls. Each one waked with a connecting bloodline. Something told me that Fae blood wasn't the only thing these mutts were breeding. None of the cats laid around as if taking a nap. No, all of them were on watch. They were sentinels. The moment something of interest happened, one would be off to share the news.

But with whom?

The question tickled the back of my neck.

The markings on the calico's were distinct enough for me to tell them apart. The black cats were a different story. Green eyes abounded. However, the first black cat I'd spotted had yellow eyes. As far as I could tell, it was the only one, and it was following me.

Out of the fog, people joined the cat-laden world of New Orleans. Most couldn't carry a shine unless someone punched them in the eye. They were human one and all, carrying baskets of fruit, vegetables, and herbs. One had a wooden box filled with bottles.

Everything a bustling town needs to survive.

Each and every one was dressed in shabby grimy clothes. There couldn't be much to burn out here on the water. And they needed fire to boil water to drink, bathe, wash. They needed to boil water literally to do anything.

Without dry ground, where do they get their food?

It dawned on me why the plantation close to the cave had been taken over, and thus, the cave found. The witches needed land to keep their little boggy shithole going.

I was so interested in what was going on, I'd missed what wasn't.

Speech!

No one was talking. No hellos, or good to see you, no whispered murmurings of life in so and so's houses. Nothing. Everything was quiet but for the lapping of water and the dripping from the poles that were lifted and lowered to move a dory.

The humans stared straight ahead, never taking in what was going on. They didn't stumble or trip. It was a quiet creepy order.

Hopping from one dock to another, my small, yellow eyed friend followed my every move. It even hitched a ride with another boat as we passed from one group of buildings to another. Cats could see through glamors. The hair on the back of my neck began to itch with a ferocity I'd not experienced since all the pixie poop hit the fan.

Not since I'd seen Puca again.

Part of me grew desperate to scratch it. Another wanted to toss a dagger, pin that cat to the deck and be done with it.

But that might bring the whole lot down on me.

Nick's magic trail still streamed through town. I glanced at the sky to gauge how much time I had left before the sun rose. It wasn't far off, so I turned my boat and poled off into the bayou, looking for somewhere to hunker down until the next day.

I thanked Danu that Nick didn't have to worry about the sun and Mabe's curse. Being the son of the first king of Fae had its perks and daylight walking was one of them. I was thankful.

He never could have saved me without it.

One of the many rotting buildings loomed in the distance. It was four stories above the water, but leaning precariously to one side.

That was it. I decided to find an interior room and wait out the light.

Even if it means I have to stay awake all day.

I docked my boat and hummed for hunter's vine to cover it, making it blend into the building. The floor shivered under my weight, and I sang for light as a feather and Jack to make me nimble. The groaning of the structure ceased. My beating heart lightened with my step, and I tiptoed my way into the darkness inside.

A few of my forest friends crowded in through the windows. They squeaked to each other about the accommodations. Some complained it was too damp to hold on to the wood, while others chose to inspect the upper levels. I wished them well on their search for a daylight resting place.

The first main problem I came to was the steel I-beam sticking up through the middle of a room. There was a gaping tear in the center of the building, where the structure pulled away from the rigid steel. The beam was as solid as the day humanity set it in the bedrock and cement. It was perfect. Everything around it was giving way. The steel waked of its integrity. It was proud to hold its form after all this time. A smirk scraped one side of my face, taking my mind off the task at hand.

Yet, that moment slipped away so quickly, it was easy to believe I'd only wished for the half-smile. The beam was the answer to my needs. I sang for the house that Jack built, pulling my body up the beam until I reached the top floor. I toed around, glancing out windows looking for a way to reach this level other than magic. I hummed a fire escape into sandy granules of the minerals it was composed of and let them slip into the bayou water surrounding us.

The building contained less iron than I expected, allowing me to breathe a sigh of relief. An apartment had an interior bathroom in decent shape. I closed the door, calling on my hunter's vine to attack anyone who came within five feet of the door, then I layered song upon song to secure the door and walls. I hummed a bubble of protection around my body.

I was as safe as I was going to be. I stepped into the bathtub and sat down to wait for the sleep that was never going to come.

Not until Nick knows that I forgave him.

I didn't want the cement block in my belly to be with me for the rest of my life just because I didn't forgive him when I had the chance.

I was a foolish Fae.

Love is the greatest hunt of all, and I fucked it all up over my pride.

I wanted to cry or scream. The pressure on my chest choked me. Instead, I stared at the door to my safe space, wishing to Danu that the sun would set, and Nick would be okay.

The safety of this room, like everything else, was an illusion.

Love is the only reality.

CHAPTER 12

SARAH

I stormed out of the throne room. The walls quaked as my feet took each step. The leaves laid flat against the stone, cowering. All the fruit withered and died, along with whatever fresh blooms had brightened my way.

The walls, unlike everyone else down here, got the fuck out of my way.

I am so over all this bullshit.

The entrance to the dungeons yawned before me. It was one of the many exits from the stair room, straight across from the golden path and to archways.

I glanced over to the main staircase. There, in a protection bubble, sat Wenn.

"Still choosing the wrong side?" I asked as I crossed the room.

"I don't take sides. I'm on my own side," he grumbled and scratched his left butt cheek while sneering at me.

"I'm removing my enemies. You have two Fae days to choose my side," I stopped and smiled at him. "Otherwise, I'm coming back to hack every limb from your body before I snatch that red blood-soaked hat from your head."

He scowled at me.

"You can leave the hat outside the bubble if you want to live," I smirked at him and kept going.

You can feel the iron long before you see the magic. It wakes through the stone, reaching for you.

Yet, I still couldn't figure out how iron could kill a Fae exactly. Yes, it worked like kryptonite, but it didn't just weaken you. It burned and cooked you from the outside in. The closer I got to it, the more it felt like I was standing next to a fire pit and the wind was blowing at me.

The stairs were much like every other castle in Fae. They really did lack imagination when I came to dungeons here. It was a winding corkscrew of a cylinder down into the ground.

The iron wasn't in the hallway or stairwell. It was only in the cells. The amount of iron in each room grew the farther away from the stairs you went, and with my level of power, I was extremely sensitive to even a tiny amount.

Healing the redness wasn't an issue. My status turned me into a healing machine. I was rarely hurt for more than a few hours, which was why the magic blast shocked me so much.

I must have been close to death.

I brushed that thought away and pushed on.

Cernunnos' deep baritone drifted out of the third door. I came to a stop in the doorway and took in the situation.

The female was naked and spread wide. Iron poker marks lay on her skin with ferocity. One mark, in particular, was crisp with blackened edges. The skin in the middle was gone, leaving only a congealed bloody blue mess to ooze from the sides.

She coughed and a little blood rimmed her lips.

"I beg for mercy, my Queen," she murmured around a swollen tongue.

"Fuck mercy! That time has passed. Don't '*My Queen*' me either. I'm over it. Talk, or I'll leave a changeling from Jacques court down here to teach you why you should never cross me before I shove you in with the slough."

I took a breath. It felt good to back up a threat with action. I hungered for the action.

"Jacques took Janice after the blast. He was dazed," she stopped to breathe.

I hummed a poker into the air and allowed it to hover over her chest.

Fae like pretty.

Wasn't that what the Fomorian told me?

"It would be a shame to make you as ugly on the outside as inside."

Her eyes rolled. She gulped back the blood pooling in her mouth. "Finian slipped him a sleeping draft, so they could whisk him away."

I lowered the poker, and she turned her face away.

"What is his plan?"

The hair framing her eyes began to melt with the heat. Her eyelashes looked like a lighter held too close to your face. If I allowed it to hang a little lower, flames might burst forth.

"He's looking for a piece of the stone well, Danu's bucket and the wand. He thinks it does something important. He will kill you to get it. He's searching all of Fae," she whimpered.

I pulled the poker back one inch.

"He's looking for Pil," the prisoner added.

"What did you tell him?" I growled. Just the simple mention of that female turned my belly.

With all the acid churning inside me, I could hardly hold my anger back. My magic wakes cut little marks into her skin.

"I told him you banished her to the surface." She bit down, and her lip began to bleed.

It was a lie. I didn't banish her. I told her she could go there if she found a way to do so without magic.

If Puca hadn't meddled, she would still be down here, looking for a way out.

And Arty would still be alive.

My nostrils flared, my chest rose with a deep breath I pulled in and pushed out. It was the only way to keep myself from crying.

Silver was in my hand. It registered that I hadn't put it away.

I trailed the sharp tip down the inside of her left thigh, and a thin line of blood welled up. She sucked in air to keep from screaming.

I was at a disadvantage. I didn't know what the bucket or the wand was, let alone what they did. A thousand questions tumbled around in my melon.

The only bucket I'd ever heard of was the one from Jack and Jill.

Janice's voice calmly told me in my mind they betrayed Danu. They climbed the hill to the well.

All the pictures from my childhood showed a wooden well with a wooden bucket hanging from a crank.

But most of the wells I'd seen were lined in stone.

My breath ran shallow. I couldn't even form the right sentence to ask about the well or the stupid bucket.

"Why did he take Janice?" It didn't make sense. Janice wouldn't know where the bucket or wand was.

"Jacques said Janice betrayed him. He chose the wrong side."

I hitched my lips to the side, "There is a lot of that going around," I murmured.

My mind wandered into this quagmire as my body wandered out of the room. I stopped to stare off into the stone. Its waking surface spoke of age.

I mindlessly tossed over my shoulder, "Shut her in, but keep her alive!"

"Yes, my Queen," the guards, who I'd hardly noticed, chimed in unison.

Without thinking, I passed through the room filled with stairs. Wenn shouted from the landing. I was so deep in thought, it didn't penetrate. I waved him off. He screamed as I entered the golden archway.

My feet took me to the library and the Record Keeper.

Lavender sat at a large table surrounded by stacks of books. She took to her feet and curtsied with a grace I didn't think I could ever have. When I finally met her eyes, I said the only thing that came to mind.

"He took Janice."

I'd meant to ask about her research or the stone well. I wanted to ask what the bucket and wand were and why Jacques would want them. Even the thought of whistling for Puca had all been there. But none of that came out.

That's why Jacques took him. To do this to me.

And it was working.

Lavender made her way around the table. She cupped my cheek, her beautiful face pinched in concern. I usually found comfort in her violet coloring and marking. Not today. She wrapped me in her arms and my chest locked with pain.

I couldn't breathe. The thought of Janice with Jacques and all the ways he could be hurt seized within me while. the overwhelming desire to throw up and pass out rolled through me. It mixed together, covering me in sweat.

For a moment, I wanted to let go. For a moment I wanted to let every feeling I carried around bottled up inside out, like popping the cork on a shaken bottle of champagne. I could even see the green of the glass as the bubble-infused alcohol shot from the opening and poured over the side.

But like that bottle, I would explode, and Jacques would win. So, instead of that, I leaned into Lavender's comforting arms, swallowing it all back and locking it into a proverbial bottle marked with '*don't drink me*'. Then, I set it on a little table in a large room next to a little locked door. The room was filled with everything I wasn't allowed to feel or do.

The life I will never have.

I pulled away from all that comfort and safety. "Show me what you've found."

CHAPTER 13

MERCIA

Cats yowled for the latter half of the daylight. It came from far off. Although they weren't here, they were looking for me. I understood their call. They were trying to rally the local animals to their cause.

Little did they know that the Flittermice started that game long before the sun breached the sky. The locals were ours. So the yowling grew, laced with frustration and getting more desperate as the hours went on until it was a full-blown caterwaul.

I had no idea if the cats knew who I was. But I was there, and they knew it. That was enough.

As soon as I get out of here, I am going to call on the local gater population and see how that goes when I throw a few cats in the water.

I smiled to myself at the vision that played through my mind. Wet cats were truly a sad sight. Plus, the growling would hit overdrive.

I sank into a dreamless sleep for a few hours only to jolt awake. The building groaned with additional weight.

Someone is here.

My feet found the floor, and I sang for all the power Jack could bestow on me, then I slapped each cheek and unslung my bow.

The hunter's vine outside the door moved with my humming as I directed them to open the ceiling of the room onto the roof. I whistled for the vines to dig their way into the walls.

If the vines take over, I will own this leaning shack of rot.

With one foot, I balanced on the edge of the tub and reached into the hole in the ceiling, grabbed onto the steel rafter, and pulled. I moved with the lightness of a feather out of the building and onto what was left of the black tar paper covering the roof.

My clothes were in several different shades, so I sang for black. The magic decided my bow would blend in as well. I wanted to blend into the shadows as much as possible. I pulled my hunter's cloak from its magical hiding place and slung it over my shoulders. I pulled the hood to hide my Fae shine. The risks were too high. I couldn't afford such a simple mistake.

What if someone is more than a quarter Fae? What if they can see the shine?

I quickly shook that idea away. That was a hunter quality, and as far as I knew, there were only two hunters ever made -Momma and Cernunnos. One for the UnSeelie and later one for the Seelie. There had to be a balance.

For the first time, it dawned on me - Sarinha, the new Queen, must've had hunter's blood.

That's why she won. Hunters don't lose.

That made her and I the only half-blood hunters in the world.

I snorted as I stepped to the edge of the roof and looked down.

Sarinha may be half hunter, but she will never be as good as me.

I emerged from my chrysalis as a hunter. I was raised to kill. She would never have that. She was born human.

The desire to gloat was lost as I took in the water on this side of the building. Dory's row boats and rafts of all varieties surrounded the building, as if the entire coven had come to say *hi*.

The part of me that was human, the part I liked to ignore, quivered in fear. On the other hand, the Fae side pulled my cheeks back into a wicked grin. I was ready for the fight.

I sure hope they are too, or this is going to be short.

This wasn't like in the forest. This time I had nothing to lose and I was ready for them. Yet, none of the faces turned my way. They couldn't see me, and that was all I needed.

I leaped off the side of the building and hummed for the vines. They slithered below the building's surface just inside the walls. The wind of my fall attempted to push the hood back from my face, but the magic held it firm.

The hunter's vine bumped out from the side of the building, and I grabbed two handholds. My feet found a place to toe in, and I turned to face the crowd of boats. Each one carried a witch and an enchanted human.

I hadn't seen their eyes before. However, a milky white film covered each and every one. They were mental slaves to the New Orleans coven.

Someone here is very powerful.

Whoever it was, wasn't on a boat in front of me. None here carried the shine. All were as watered down as the land under our feet. What they carried were charms and pouches and trinkets. These were worthless against me. The charms waked with the leftover power of a long-dead changeling.

Not even a real Fae.

The pouches were filled with bones and hair. They pilfered their dead.

My stomach roiled with the idea. Momma said that the Savannah witches did the same thing. They had generations of witches' blood and bones to pull from. The Haggs of Savannah never knew what was coming.

I needed to whittle their numbers down. So, I pulled an Alice song. It played on my mind all day, and now it was about to play across my lips.

"How doth the little crocodile,

Improve his shining tail?"

Pairs of bumps appeared from the water. Each reptile blinked to adjust its sight for the dry air.

"And pour the waters of the Nile,

On every golden scale!"

The narrow slits of their irises widened, allowing more light to reach the cornea at the center of their golden eyes. The tips of their noses breached the water without a sound.

My smile grew, and I waited for the rest of my reptilian friends to join us. They didn't care that I'd called them crocodiles, and they were alligators. To them, the call was the same. Magic and intent are all that was needed to cast a spell. Not trinkets and charms.

"How cheerfully he seems to grin."

Mouths opened a fraction of an inch.

"How neatly spreads his claws,

And welcomes little fishes in,

With gently smiling jaws!"

Their mouths burst open from the water as their tails whipped back and forth, pushing their upper body out and onto the boat. Those jaws snapped closed on whatever body they were closest to. Then, like the weight of an anvil, they stole their prize. Sinking down into the depths, they disappeared.

And oh, such screams arose.

It was new, delicious music to my ears. I sang for Fae fire and burned all the charms and trinkets I'd laid eyes on. Whatever witches left on my side of the building were powerless.

Rather than reveal my location, I pulled my bow and began shooting as I moved along the side of the building. I met the corner, and the hunter's vine hung before me, like a vine in the jungle.

I tied it around my waist and kicked off, swinging far out over the water and shooting at my prey from above. I stopped just as the swing met its crest. The trip back to the building took forever. I was on the short side of the structure. I tiptoed to the next corner and peeked around. This was the high side of the building, opposite from where I'd started. The vine around my waist grew longer, allowing me to walk down the outside wall closer to the water. The witches on this side were stronger than the others.

That was a mistake.

They should have peppered the strong in with the weak.

Not... My... Problem.

I squatted and took a beat to take in this next group before the volley began.

They were older, with more magical changes. The charms were the same, only stronger. Plus, they carried more of them.

There were layers of spells over the boats to keep projectiles out and others to keep them afloat. It was a joke. The spells were woven together by a child that barely understood the technique.

It was actually kind of sad.

Such a waste.

Even the witches and warlocks of my old stomping grounds could have put up a better fight.

My mind flashed to Cassidy holding me against a wall and telling everyone I belonged to him. My nostrils flared. I didn't belong to anyone but myself. For a split second, Nick rolled through my head, and then right back out.

Not now!

The sure shot bow would do its job. My arrows just needed a pick-me-up. I pulled three bolts and hummed over them, turning the tips into a magic knife. They could cut the loose weave of the song and slip right through.

My body took to its full height, and I dashed this way and that, shooting as I went, never standing in one place. As I loosed an arrow, I moved the moment it left my fingers. I was almost at the next corner.

An old witch raised something and screeched.

"The shadow!"

The moonlight spilled across the building, outing me. The shadow cloak only worked in the gloom and darkness. Direct light of any kind turned me into a moving shadow.

I dove for the corner of the building. I tossed the Fae fire song over my shoulder as I went. I had enough time to catch a glimpse of what the woman was holding. It was a light of some kind from before.

Lightning crashed into the side of the building, burning a hole where my leg had been. The hunter's vine in the wall curled in on itself in pain.

The pain filtered back to me, and my side burned with it. The vine around my waist still held. Yet, I needed a quick exit. There were too many to face head-on. My element of surprise was spent, and I needed to regroup.

I sang for the alligators again and watched as they pulled a fresh meal from the boats.

Some of the witches banished the watery beasts back. The distraction was too much for others. The Fae fire engulfed them and their boat along with their human pet.

I pushed off the building, swinging into the shadow of a nearby tree. The witches landed several hits on the building. The hunter's vine cried out from the attacks.

I stumbled in answer to the attacks at the base of the banyan tree. This was a mistake. I should have pulled my vines back.

Pixie shit!

I snapped my finger at the vine around my waist. The tendril disintegrated.

The pain lancing my side grew sharper, and I turned to protect the weakness. My heart hammered in my chest. I pulled back against the tree and whistled reaching its roots. I ordered them to part, creating a dark hollow in which to crouch.

"Mon petite, we rule here. You will not leave this bayou alive without my permission. Your man is mine. You should give him up." The voice came across stronger than I expected. Although, the lilt of youth was gone. She sounded very old. Maybe even old enough to remember the time before the fall.

Silly mutt! I will never lash out just because you have something I want.

More boats arrived, and with them, more witches. This was no longer a good field of battle.

The old woman waved to the building. Boats moved forward, and members of the coven entered the building. I waited for all who wanted to die to join the party.

The vine backlash of pain grew, and when I knew they were deep enough, I snapped my fingers.

The building pulled in on itself. It shifted back and forth as the structure fought the inevitable.

Clever vines!

They pulled like a hunter, leaving no evidence of what happened. The vines pulled here and retreated there. The structure shivered and fell all at once into the murky depths.

I took the distraction for myself and dove into the dark water. I sang for the breath of life and swam under the boats clustered around the fallen apartment building.

The light from the old woman flashed over the water. The bodies of witches were fighting to free themselves from the building. Yet, instead of help from above, death came from below. Fish swan from the darkness. Some took small bites while others pummeled the witches, breaking the skin.

With such rich red blood in the water, more predators would come. I kicked my legs to move me beyond the feeding frenzy that was only getting started.

An alligator moved alongside me. I grabbed onto his shoulder and allowed him to pull me along. He led me back to the heart of town. All the iron under the water waked, informing me of its burning presence. The dark brown water clogged my throat as a fit of panic took over.

I let go of the gator and pushed back. The gator stopped and turned to eye me. I shook my head. He didn't understand. The iron was nothing more than a barrier to him.

Fresh welts grew on my skin. It was coming from either side of the space between the underwater buildings.

A choking sensation took over, then clawing at my neck. The memory of my toes burning with iron filled my senses, I clasped my feet in fear.

My heart hammered in my chest. I couldn't push the memory back. It filled my world. Just as the water surrounded me, the iron, too, was everywhere.

For a moment, I was back in that iron box. I scrunched my eyes closed to protect them from the pain, hoping I wouldn't go blind. The burning took over my mind, and it became the world I lived in. The past and present were mixing together into a gooey mess.

A blow landed in my belly, pushing me back and knocking all the watery air from my chest. My eyes popped open, the gator's nose was buried in my stomach. He was pushing me backward.

The pain of the blow cleared my mind as if I'd slapped my face. Although, reality slammed into me harder than the gator ever could.

I will never make it through that town.

I needed help.

CHAPTER 14

SARAH

The Record Keeper lingered along a wall. Something told me it was taller than I was being led to believe. The faded yellow markings on its hands were more mustard than lemon, leaving them with a jaundiced effect.

I shivered to think age could do that to a Fae. The long hair that peeked from under the cowl was a stringy version of hay. The color lacked luster. Yet, the aura surrounding the creature was very much alive. There was no sign of impending death.

"Sarinha?" Lavender inquired as her brows pinched in concern.

I wasn't losing focus. I wasn't.

The record keeper bothered me, and I couldn't say why. It was either that or I was traveling down that river once known as the de-Nile.

I snorted. Neither the river nor the country it once was associated with existed anymore.

The Fae took that too.

The taste of hysteria is sweet but not a good type of sweet. It's sticky and overpowering. It hits you so hard that instead of enjoying the experience, you reject it. You only swallow because you think it won't hurt you. It's the cotton candy of childhood times, three thousand to the power of eight. Throw a caramel candy in the mix, and you have hysteria.

Once you swallow it, it's too late to go back.

My throat wanted to swallow. That is its normal function. But I couldn't allow that to happen. The mental war started on the tip of my tongue and raced throughout my body, tripping over the bottles I had lying everywhere of all the things I couldn't feel or share - the proof that I was alone in the struggle.

So, instead of swallowing the hysteria this time, calmly, I stepped away from Lavender. I spit the emotion onto the cold stone floor. It melted into the tight space between the stones.

"Begin!" I ordered with a stronger voice than I thought I had. The very act of spitting the feeling out, freed me of it. That outcome would need to be investigated.

But not now.

"I wasn't sure what you wanted me to read first, so I started with how Jacques was freed." She glanced up at me through the bangs hanging in her eyes.

Her hair, for once, was black, and the sharp contrast of her violet eyes and pale skin was breathtaking.

"Finian left you and immediately entered the throne room. He whispered something the walls couldn't hear. He kissed Jacques' palm and sliced Deston's wrists."

The pages of the book moved with her words to display the actions. It was similar to Cernunnos.

I brought him close to death. They shared a kiss before I healed him.

*****

The broken torc on Jacques' wrist lost its waking magic and released Jacques. Deston lay on the edge of death.

"Master, my brother?" Finian petted Deston's face. A single tear traced its way down a cheek before falling on Deston's cheek, the perfect reflection of his own.

He made no move to save him, even though he was capable. The love he felt for his brother was unmistakable.

"Leave him! Your brother is of no use to me."

Finian choked. The aura around Deston bled away with his life. The magic of an oath held Finian back from his heart's desire. The binds of an oath grew tighter with each second until Deston was dead. The roar of agony and loss loosed from Finian's body as Janice entered the room.

"If only I'd been wrong," Janice growled. He dove for Jacques, choosing the great danger of the two.

Jacques batted him away like a fly. He sang for the London bridge to fall down and lock Janice up. The magic chains tightened around Janice's neck and body, cutting off any chance at singing himself free. A moment later, the magic slammed him into the stone floor.

"A warrior is no match for a prince."

Jacques smiled and tapped the end of Janice's nose. "She should have chosen you for King. You'd be trapped but *alive. Now, you won't want to be alive for long," he chuckled and snapped his fingers, forcing Janice's body to rise off the floor.*

Finian wept softly next to his twin's body. "He didn't need to die."

"Stop the milk sopping! Deston failed me. Don't follow in your brother's steps. Bring your cousin, and for your sake, I hope he doesn't get free." He cocked an eyebrow at the crouched form, "I don't think you'd live long." Jacques strutted out of the throne room as the conquering hero.

He glanced left and right, then took the left-hand course to the library.

*****

My throat closed with the invisible chain around Janice's neck. His eyes bulge over the strain to breathe and the desire to hum, or sing.

He isn't strong enough.

I slammed the book, making the Record Keeper squeak. I shot it with a glare. "Show me what he read."

Lavender whistled the dust from a chair for me and indicated I should sit. It was an invitation, even though for the outside eye, it might have looked otherwise. Lavender, always mindful of how things might be perceived, bowed low in respect.

If anyone else had done it, I would have slammed them into the floor and made them lick the dust from the cracks. Yet, I understood Lavender's ways. She was too familiar. I couldn't bring myself to rebuff her. I needed someone who wasn't afraid of me. Even my mother was scared.

Janice knows I would never hurt him. Nick too.

The only person not afraid and who literally was not give two fucks was Puca. Why he was different, I couldn't figure out.

My father was once King, yet he didn't retain the powers of King. He was no more Fae than the day he took the crown. He was a prince and nothing more. On the other hand, Puca was a riddle.

Am I as strong as him or stronger?

I carried his blood and so did Nick.

Now that was one person I didn't need to worry about. Dear old Uncle Nick was safe on the surface, and the only person who knew where he was, was Puca.

Just like my mother.

Puca would never give them up. Nikki was enough for him.

Lavender rearranged the table and placed two books in front of me. Each was made with a substance I'd never seen before.

I picked up the first volume and turned it over. I glanced around the room to make sure it wasn't a joke, then moved my focus back to the book. It was covered in leather, but it wasn't attached. It was just a covering.

I quickly set it down and grabbed the next book. It, too, had a leather covering. They were exactly the same. My mouth dried.

There was no way these books could be thousands of years old. They were machine stitched. The pages were a perfect even cut. However, they were made from a fiber I'd never seen before. The leather was the skin of an unknown animal.

I pulled the books free of their holders. The word *acta observatio* was printed on the front. Inside, there were more words I didn't know.

Observatio sounded like *observe*.

Journal— observe?

I flipped through more pages until I came across a word I did know -*Terra*. Land, dirt, earth! It was Latin.

Latin is a dead language.

It was kind of dead before the fall and totally dead now.

Why would a book thousands of years older than Latin be written in Latin?

"Lavender, can you read this?"

She nodded her head, and her eyes grew wide. "Yes, my Queen. This is the language of Fae in its pure form. Just as Danu taught us."

The keeper sighed and kept its distance. I narrowed my eyes and shot it a searing glare.

"What does this sentence say?" I pointed to the word *terra*.

"This land is unlike my home. It is filled with the mineral, and I can use it."

What mineral?

Lavender shrugged when I looked at her. "Jacques was inspecting a different part of the book. If I may," she opened her hand so I could give her the book.

It was a modern-looking book. Amazon could have shipped it to my house before the fall. Only the front would probably have said something like diary, journal, or composition.

Reluctantly, I relinquished the prize, and she quickly flipped back to the early pages in the book. Lavender laid the book in front of me and pointed to a paragraph. "That is where he started."

"I can't read Latin," I groused and pushed the offending item back at her.

She leaned over and pointed to each word as she read.

"I have finished tuning the resonance of each stone and believe that my next set of chords will be the one. I can't wait to see where the circle will lead me. Wherever it is, it will be a new world, and I will be its master."

My mouth dried.

A new world?

Resonance was not a word used by Fae. I had been down there long enough to know that. They didn't tune things. It just happened. To them, a tune was a song, not the note itself.

If your magic didn't work, it was because you didn't sing it right. Fae would use the word tone or vibration, not resonance.

"What else does it say? What did he read?" I demand. My hand grabbed the other book, and I quickly turned pages, looking for more words I knew.

Studium leaped from the page.

Thank God most English words have some kind of a Latin base word.

Studium had the word study in it. She was studying something, and it changed her world. She tuned the resonance of a circle of stones.

Oh my God!

She created the stones. They weren't natural.

There can be more, so many more.

The adrenaline from my kills froze in my veins. If ever there was a time for Google Translate, now would be it.

CHAPTER 15

MERCIA

The song for breathing underwater was only good to use once every 24 hours. Magic does have limits. I had to remind myself of that. The song would wear off.

My watery friend pushed me deep into the bayou. I sat on the muddy beachhead, next to a shack, coughing at the water still lingering in my lungs.

The bank was lined with gators, all relaxing. Most of them looked to be sleeping. That was a trick. Every living creature has a trick to lure their kill. Gators and crocs lay in wait. Whether they are on land or in the water. They, like cats, could be incredibly still. Even the eyes cease to move.

I sat up, and immediately, a flittermouse swooped down on me. It was the old-timer who chirped with excitement, claiming the battle had been a success.

I ran my hands over my body, taking in all the burn marks and reddened skin. I couldn't agree, yet I let him go. He claimed fifteen witches perished in the '*building battle*'.

Even the title is a joke.

I was damn lucky to get out of there alive and free. Pulling the building down was the only thing that saved me. The gators didn't need me to do anything but coordinate. They did most of the work.

I sat there trying to regroup in my mind. I needed more arrows. Calling back the ones I'd use was too dangerous. I couldn't go into that town alone, and my pets weren't enough.

If the flittermice believed that fight was a win, we were well, and truly Fae fucked.

The gators were happy to have a few good meals for the next few weeks. I grimaced at the thought of eating old bloated human meat for weeks.

Yuck!

A gator nudged me. His nose was clammy. The breath coming out of it was moist and warm. It was no different from any other animal but still a little gross.

Focusing on the shortcomings of my allies was a lesson in stupidity. Yes, they had weaknesses, but strengths too.

The flittermice could travel at night and scout quietly while the gators were able to move at any time unnoticed.

What *I need is a magic-user.*

In my heart of heavy hearts, no matter the cost, I knew who I had to call.

My master would want to know. Not to save Nick.

Who am I kidding?

I was the only one interested in that.

No, he will want the bowl.

Puca would never deviate from his mission, whatever that was. He would chide me for wasting time. Yet, it won't be more than I chided myself.

If I haven't been so wrapped up in punishing Nick...

I took to my feet and moved back from the water's edge, then pressed my lips together and blew.

The sound of Puca's whistle was not a foreign one. Just one I'd never made myself. The sense of fear that waked through me as the notes spilt the air, knocked the breath from my lungs. The visage in front of me shook and shivered before splitting in two. Puca's portal formed out in the human reality, and he stepped through. The scent of leather, male, and horse came through with him.

I took a step back. Puca's sharp eyes cut me to the core, "Where is my son?" He demanded. There was none of his prancing around. No words gamed. Only the cold unadulterated anger that comes with an unforeseen consequence.

The gray wakes turned into fists the size of boulders, eager to punish me.

I dropped to my knees and quickly crossed my fingers and arm before touching my chest.

"Master, I should have listened to you," I gulped the sour taste back and the apology that went with it. Saying sorry wouldn't fix the problem, only action would.

"The New Orleans Witches were there in force with a circle and broke the song, holding the bowl safe. The blast from the spell knocked me senseless, and they took Nick." I couldn't meet his canary yellow eyes. My tale was too common to be forgiven. Not becoming of an elite assassin.

Momma would never have been caught at such a loss. Shame rolled over me because Puca knew that to be true.

"What do you need to succeed?" He asked through gritted teeth.

My mouth dried. I had to ask, and there would be a price. Whatever the price was, I would have to pay it. He already owned my body and sword as the keeper.

What more will he take?

"I cannot reach the city. There is too much iron in the water. The buildings are riddled with it. I am too Fae to make the trip. I need a helper, an underling." It was a safe ask.

Someone with just enough Fae to sing but not enough to be burned by the iron.

"I will provide you what you need." He slicked his hair back and paced around the embankment. The animals sidestepped to make way.

A flittermouse landed on his shoulder and whispered of our battle success. I gazed down at the water before me, keeping my face as blank as possible. When I finally chanced a glance at Puca, his eyebrow was lifted in mock sunrise.

"You used an Alice song?" he crossed his arms and planted his feet on the moist ground.

"Yes, Master," I replied and looked away. The heat of shame raced over me anew. Alice songs were for the weakest of Fae, those with little blood and even less power.

"Brush up on the Alice songs. You are going to need them," he growled.

He ripped the air open and stepped through the portal. The magic slammed shut, pushing my hair back. I slumped to the ground. Even the gnawing in my belly couldn't rouse me.

Puca didn't ask for his payment, but the price was coming. Unlike the last time I swore an oath to him, I understood the price would be high, so very high.

My eyes burned as if being dug out with iron. I had one job, to keep the wand and the bowl safe from everyone.

And I failed.

The burning inside ignited my skin. I ripped my leather jerkin and shirt open to expose my chest and screeched at the top of my lungs until my throat was as raw as the burn marks on my body.

The gators growled, and the bayou came alive. Every creature heard my call of pain, anger, and frustration. They all screamed with me, their deafening roar filling me with resolve.

CHAPTER 16

MERCIA

There was still plenty of time until daylight to find a hidie hole, looking seemed irrelevant.

The shack I shared the bank with sat in quiet decline. I called for my hunter's vine to secure it. The flittermice chirped in approval. I left them a small opening. They would scare the humans away.

The coven must know by now that I am in congress with the flittermice.

The vines twined around the shack, engulfing the windows. I whistled for a banyan tree to grow around the structure, hiding it from the prying eyes of the living. The tree would hide the magic of my hunter's vine and keep the daylight out.

The magic settled, yet I found I couldn't move. The choice to warn the flittermice was a rock that joined all the rest of my problems that were lying in my belly.

The coven would begin killing every flittermouse in the bayou and marshes. They would decimate the bat population in this area until none remained.

The building battle was the first salvo in a bigger war they were now a part of.

With no one to observe me, I bit my lip. Vacillating was not the hunter's way, nor would a Fae stand still for such indecision.

I called the old flittermouse to me and whispered my concerns.

He laughed it off and said the witches search for magic, not cunning. His assertion of flittermice cunning was humorous. I didn't dissuade him of the belief. Instead, I sent him on his way. The bat population could rise or fall on their own choices.

I sat waiting on the bank for hours before the dawn of a new day forced me into the safe harbor of the shack.

Sleep never came. The night went, and a new day came without Puca or contact of any kind. I retreated to the shack in daylight and rocked myself, hoping for sleep and finding only the hot eyes of worry.

The visions of Nick being tortured or worse never stopped their dance in my imagination.

When night fell, I decided to leave. The witches would believe I was dead by now and have returned to their regularly scheduled plans.

Puca can find me wherever I may be.

I called a gator to my side and entered the water.

"You would go alone?" Puca's voice cleaved the air.

I whirled around to face him.

"I go for him, the bowl, and to reverse my failure," I shouted, and it bounced back off the water. "Master," I added it as an afterthought.

"I have found what you asked for," he replied as his eyes burned the red of a hot fire. The scent of wolf rose around us. His face carried the fur of a change. It slowly receded back into his form, as did sharp canine teeth.

He was alone, and I glanced up and down the bank to assure myself of the fact.

"I asked for a weak changeling. Where is the halfling?" my arms crossed, and I cocked a hip out. I was playing a dangerous game.

But life is dangerous.

The wakes around the one-time King erupted in violence. In a flash, he was in my face, the long teeth touching my skin. "You dare to question me, when you have failed worse than any before you?" he shouted. His head pushed into mine, and I coward.

The magic cut me, making me bleed.

Most of his body was shaped like the wild dog he could become, yet he stood erect.

"You will not leave this patch of dirt until I return. You will retrieve the stone bowl, and my son. if you can. Then and only then will you be back in my good graces. I will not tolerate your failure. If you die, I will give your body to the slough, and you will never rest. By Danu's love, I still rule here." His breath heaved, hot and moist in my face.

I turned my head, offering the back of my neck.

"What…" I started but had to stop to swallow back the vitriol at the top of my throat, "What if I can't save Nick?" tears flooded my eyes. I gritted my teeth to keep my cries at bay. He could sense my feeling and my wavering resolve over the bowl.

"Then you will do what I did - leave your heart behind. We have a higher calling than love," he growled.

My body shivered. He huffed, and a drop of saliva fell on my neck. He then shoved me to the ground. "Go in your shack and wait." The air behind him ripped open, and he stepped back into the Hallowed Hills.

I caught a glimpse of a garden and the sound of falling water a second before the portal slammed shut.

I tipped onto my side and curled into a ball to cry.

When your master gives you an order, you cannot disobey.

No matter what I did, Nick wasn't my priority, and I couldn't change that. The magic would force me to leave without him if the opportunity presented itself.

I couldn't recount my oath to Puca. Humanity needed me. Ron needed me. Shea needed me. Every changeling needed me. Humanity was my first priority, and Puca made the bowl the key to fulfilling that.

No matter which way I turned, I was trapped. My vision filled with a blurred version of the banyan tree, cloaking my shack.

The magic pulled at me to return to its safety. I pulled my body from the muddy bank and let the magic lead me inside.

Pacing. I like to pace.

The hunter's blood desires movement. Momma paced too. Whenever she was trapped in a room or underground during the day she paced. Sometimes she went weeks without sleeping. She sucked on roots to keep herself awake. I had no such roots.

I laid my tools on the floor - one bow with a quiver full of bolts, three-finger daggers, and my long barrel rifle. The bullets waked with the magic of sure shot. It was a form of cheating, sort of.

My clothes were filthy. I hummed them clean. It was an Alice song. The grime disappeared from my hair, leaving the tips white. I was changing courts, and I didn't care.

Courts are for the Fae trapped underground.

The Seelie or UnSeelie, autumn, or winter, summer, spring… what they were, it made no difference for me. I had only one affiliation, and he didn't care what side you were on as long as you did as you're told.

Puca.

Just thinking of his name made me want to spit. He enraged me.

Now, I understand momma's hatred.

Puca could twist a flower into poison and get you to take it with a smile.

I ran down all the Alice songs and shivered. Puca said I would need them. Most were for cleaning or to fight serpents. How I could take on an entire coven with those was beyond me.

My only choice was to save Nick first.

If I can.

CHAPTER 17

Sarah

What I learned from the books shook me to my core. Danu was a clever woman. She never wrote down the resonance chords. She kept that to herself.

Unconsciously, I thanked her. That small bit of foresight might have saved us all. That was until I came to the missing page.

"Where is the wall book for the time Jacques was reading this?" I demanded.

The Record Keeper handed me a new book. But that page was gone too. I scowled up at the hooded figure.

"You have one job…"

"I am to keep the records, not protect them," the oily voice replied.

"Likely excuse. Honestly, what fuck good are you?" I couldn't get over the word games.

Every time you think you've covered all your bases, a Fae comes along to throw a wrench in that idea.

I wanted to hurt the keeper. What good it would do other than assuage an irritation, I couldn't say.

I went back and forth. The pages on either side gave no specifics away as to what their missing sister held.

She speaks of a mineral she calls magicus… sometimes magicum…

It sounded a little like magnesium. She said it was everywhere here.

The Hallowed Hills.

She could tap into it and use it to create.

Whatever the mineral was, it was the reason we could use magic.

And now Jacques knows something about it that I don't.

The *what* and *where* fore's made me crazy.

I snapped the book closed with a flourish. I didn't have time to read thousands of years of Danu's long-forgotten journals.

Lavender looked up from her tome with wide eyes.

"It's time for me to go face my King," I announced.

She pushed her chair back as if to join me.

I raised a hand, "Don't! I need you here. Keep reading. Maybe you will find something. Get help you can trust." I stopped and turned to take the cavernous room in, then ordered, "Get my mother!"

Lavender scowled at me before schooling her face. "I know not where she may be."

That was Lavender's way of saying *I can't stand the bitch and don't want to work with her.*

Lavender's kind heart would never extend to my mom. She'd decided long ago that what happened to Cernunnos was Alice's fault. However, I wasn't interested in the petty conflict between the two.

We were at war with Jacques and whatever he had planned. I needed my most trusted people working on this.

I rolled my eyes away from Lavender. She would do as I asked to a point. And getting Alice was the point.

Licking my lips, I whistled for the one person who knew where Alice was - Puca.

The wall to the library shivered and shifted like the water on a pond, then split, opening a portal. Puca stepped through with raised eyebrows.

He took in the dusty room filled with books and ran a finger across a shelf and the spine of a book or two.

"You called, granddaughter?" he arched an eyebrow at me, then shuffled a few steps in the room. From there, he raised his head and sniffed the air. After that, he whirled around to look at the Record Keeper. The Keeper retreated into the far reaches of the room, behind shelves. The sound of its robe dragging across the floor was the only thing informing us of its continued presence.

"Keep that creature away from me," he growled.

Now it was my turn to be shocked.

"Noted. Where is my mother?" I asked without preamble.

"Why? What do you need Alice for? She isn't any use to Fae. She is mine." He pivoted toward Lavender and cocked his head to the side. The gray aura around him flared with mischief.

Lavender stared up at him, then placed her hands in her lap.

"Are you following all my instructions?" he asked.

With her face reddened, she responded, "Yes."

"Yes, what? I want my granddaughter to understand."

"Yes, master!" She hung her head, and her aura's wakes changed from violet to the pink of shame.

"Is she your plaything?" I asked.

I knew the answer, but I wanted to hear him say it. I wanted to hear him say that she was only following his orders and not mine, that without demanding oaths I would have no idea to whom someone really answered to. Just like he'd told me.

My eyes narrowed, and my nose sneered. "Is there anyone you don't have twisted up in knots?" I asked. My arms were crossed, and I uncrossed them.

"What do you need Alice for? Why should I endanger her?" He touched one of my arms.

It caused a shiver to run down my spine.

Having her here, in the library, wouldn't endanger her.

"I need more eyes to read Danu's journals," I remarked and stepped away from him before he could whisper in my ear and begin his manipulations.

His charisma started with a whisper, then he'd dance around to entrance you, yadda, yadda. That shit game wouldn't work on me. His wakes around the room gave his game away.

My first instinct was to shove him to the floor. Yet, Puca Oberon couldn't be pushed around. He bit back.

"It isn't your choice, and you can't keep her from me. I will find her and ask her myself. This was a courtesy call," I snickered.

Whistle, call... same, same.

"Touche, little one. Yes, I will ask her if she wants to read dusty old books about a long-dead Fae," he laughed and ripped the wall open.

"No thanks. I'll ask her myself," I remarked and stepped through the portal to his cottage.

The room was right out of a book - soft comfy chairs and sofas, a tea table, floral prints on the furniture and walls. Outside the windows, there was a garden filled with flowers. The garden resembled any English garden on the surface.

All waked with normalcy.

In between the flower beds, my mother kneeled. Her dress was brown, and her hair hung in braids down either side of her head. She sat back on her feet and glanced over toward the cottage.

She cleaned her hands on her apron and took to her feet. Before I could stop myself, I'd flashed halfway to her. But then, I stopped.

I didn't want to look too eager. No one here knew she was alive or what she looked like. That was keeping her safe.

I lingered in the shadow of the doorframe, just out of sight from the prying eyes of Fae. A moment later, our eyes met.

Her kind smile fruited into the full shine of Fae. Her face carried the shadow of markings.

She won't be able to hide who and what she is for much longer.

It made me sad. She, too, like Lavender, never wanted more than what life had given her, to begin with.

But the magic of Fae could not be denied. The longer you existed, and the more you used magic, the more Fae you became, until there was nothing else but what you were always supposed to become.

The magic cannot be stopped. Its march is complete.

"Sarinha!" It was all she said before she stepped through the door.

I closed us off from the rest of Fae. She cupped my face and leaned over to lay a light kiss on either cheek.

"You look tired. Father told me he healed you the other day. Why? Where is Janice?" She bit her lip when she realized there was the problem.

"I need you." It was all I could get out.

"Of course. Let me change." She moved to the stairs.

I snapped my finger and hummed for her clothes to rearrange into a more appropriate dress.

Her head whipped around, "You know I don't like that."

"I don't have time for anything that I can do faster with magic. Jacques is free. Did Puca tell you that?"

The color drained from her face.

"No, he left that part out." Her eyes stared over my head at the Fae behind me.

"We shouldn't waste time. Whatever he has planned, can't be good."

I ripped open a portal back to the library. Mom stepped through with me following after her. After that, I closed the opening in Puca's face. Yet, he tore into the fabric of the air in the library right behind me. His eyes glowed red, and his nostrils flared with smoke.

"Sarinha, I must speak with you," he wasn't disrespectful. Nonetheless, it came across like a demand.

"What do you want?" I asked while waving a hand.

Puca grabbed me by the hand and drug me across the library, past several shelves until we were well away from Lavender and my mother.

"Someone gave you a red stone," he whispered, but not in my ear.

My brows pulled down.

How does he know that?

I rolled my eyes. Of course, he knew. Puca had eyes everywhere. Most Fae are probably sworn to serve him in some fashion. The ring was a real problem, and he, too, understood the seriousness of it.

"Yes," was all I could push out.

"I need it." His low voice tickled my nose hairs with vibrations.

"Why should I give it to you?" I was terrified that the thing would steal my magic and my life. "You can't use it on my mother." It was the first thought that came to mind - I imagined that he would pull the Fae from her blood to keep her forever on the edge between Fae and humanity.

And mom would let him.

She didn't want to be Fae. She didn't want to be human. She just wanted to live.

"I don't need it for her, and I would never offer her that choice. I only want her to live as a Fae. She is all I have left of Demelza. I won't sacrifice her!" He growled and his eyes glowed the golden yellow of a burning sun.

He was in his earnest. His love for my mother was a shining light in his otherwise dark world. He loved her. She was his anchor, the only weakness I could find in his devil-may-care shaped armor.

"Nick. I need it to help him," He hissed. His wakes grew violent to the point of a dark gray bordering on black. His eyes flared blood red. The hair on his head spread from his temples, down his cheeks and over his hands.

He gripped my arms.

The fear that gripped him, bled into me. "Where is Nick?" I demanded. My worry coated my throat and soured my breath.

What the fuck? Has the whole world gone to shit in three days?

"Give me the stone," Puca growled.

This was the first time he had ever asked me for anything. The words were out before I could give them a second thought. "What will you give me?"

His shirtless chest heaved. He allowed one hand to turn into a vicious claw, and he scraped the nails across his chest.

"I will end the war," he snarled.

"Not good enough. I already know that," I snapped in irritation.

I could ask for anything, including his allegiance.

He snapped his quickly, changing jaws at me. The shadow of a hare rolled over his features along with the eyes of a horse. He was losing control. I had him.

But what should I do with him?

"What do you want?" he retorted through elongated teeth and dripping saliva.

Then it hit me.

Who would Danu trust with her greatest achievement, something that would change the world?

"Give me the stone circle." My belly turned over.

I really am one of them.

If I was still human, I'd have turned the ring over to him in a heartbeat to save Nick.

No. Now, I'm all Fae.

There was no humanity left in me. The stone throne burned it away. No matter what, there was a price, and I'd just asked for the ultimate one.

Puca's aura flipped through a thousand shades of gray and green, before stopping on one - the color of a green field in the bright sun.

It must be his real color.

That was who he really was, deep down under all that gray, all that pain and bravado.

"I, Puca Oberon, first and one time King of Fae of the Hallowed Hills, give you Sarinha, Queen of Fae, the stone circle of Danu to protect for all time," with that his body slumped to the floor. It was as if the weight of a burden was removed.

A movement behind him caught my eye. The Record Keeper shifted quickly and hid behind a shelf. One nostril curled up in a half sneer at the unwelcome watcher.

"I accept the stone circle. I, Sarinha, Queen of Fae, will loan you the red stone for one fortnight in surface time and no more. You may not use it against me."

"I swear!" Puca's voice barely reached me from the floor. He bowed before me, exposing his neck. His supplication struck me as wrong.

Guilt gripped me. He was so proud, and without a moment's thought, I'd laid him low.

He raised his head a devilish smile played over his lips.

"You are learning. I will tell you where the stones are. But don't move them as it's not safe."

The guilt quickly disappeared with his remarks. I didn't want to play this game - the game that all Fae play, with their rhythmic twisting of words. But I liked to win, and this was the only way.

I glanced around and since the walls were listening, I said, "Not here."

CHAPTER 18

MERCIA

The sun went down, and Puca didn't appear. I paced in my hidey-hole where I recounted my weapons and supplies. I sang for food and let the flittermice in and out.

The gators sunned themselves during the day and snacked at night, each doing their part to help me. My bayou spies took turns, watching the watery city. There was no sign of Nick. The witches went about their business, whatever that was, while the human slaves toiled under the yoke of magic. Nothing changed for days.

Puca was in Fae.

It should take him less than an hour there to get me what I need.

Yet, for me, weeks went by and I was unable to leave my treehouse.

My pacing wore a path on the floorboards. I screamed until my throat was raw from boredom and frustration. Hunger raged in my belly, and it wouldn't be quenched.

I didn't want food. That was easy to coax into a trap or conger. I wanted the hunt. I craved the freedom to free Nick.

Every day, the pressure to return the bowl grew, turning the command of my master into something more important than my feelings. He commanded me to retrieve the bowl before he commanded me to stay here. If he didn't return soon, the magic would begin to eat away at me until there was nothing left. Rather than let that march begin, I took matters into my own hands.

'The worms go in, and the worms go out' song rang over the water. I used that song to pull back the roots of my tree. The song was about an oak, but banyan trees can be just as strong.

Their roots are so numerous, it would take a human to kill them.

After the roots were free of the bank, I sang for *'hot cross buns,'* and the magic wove them into a boat bottom.

I called on my Alice song for the gators to push the tree into the bayou after lacing it with *'light as a feather'*. Then, I called on Jack to make us all nimble and quick.

The cloak of darkness was my only friend, and I opened the shack door, so I could direct my floating palace. It was no different than calling a round.

The tree was too top-heavy, and I had to sing '*light as a feather*' three times to lighten the crown.

The city light pierced the gloom far beyond, giving the fog that lingering halo.

I've read about the human idea of Angles. It was stupid really. They probably saw a Fae and thought it was something else.

Regular humans have a hard time processing magic and explaining it. And since the shine of a Fae resembled a halo, rather than thinking of fairies, someone said Angle.

And that was the end of that.

I knew that halos were only light refracting off of mist-filled air because momma explained all human weaknesses to me. I still believed some of it. Others she was dead wrong about.

Humans are every bit as dangerous as Fae.

The tree lurched to one side, and I sang to level it out.

If we tip over at this point and went into the water, I am Fae-fucked for sure.

The tree would never move again. I would need to force-grow the shack above the waterline.

The flittermice swarmed around the branches of the tree and settled in for the ride. The old-timer chirped about the goings-on with the witches and had heard screams from a large building that smelled of blood.

A vision of that human drilling into my hip bone roared to life. The high-pitched whine of the drill just before it touched the hard bone deafened me.

Ring around the roses played in my mind. The desire to let the notes slip past my tongue teased me and the only cooling force to my rage was the number of humans it would kill. All those entranced people, the children, would die alongside the witches. I would kill the entire city if I were to sing it. I pressed my eyes closed to push the vision back along with the need.

I can't kill kids. I don't want to kill kids. A hunter protects children at all costs. It is our main purpose.

Jacques wanted us to kill and Puca changed that mandate to protect.

Either way, I can't mindlessly kill kids.

Nick would be okay. I was almost sure that they weren't going to bleed him dry. They needed him to breed. I only hoped that it was the old-fashioned kind and not the Govs' brand of breeding.

With these thoughts in mind, I called on Jack to quicken the pace.

Water is not thicker than blood but it's just as powerful.

I could bend the rules of nature all I wanted, but without the help of an element, I was stuck at the best speed I could make.

Aqualis couldn't cross into the human world. The roads built before the fall worked like a road sign, pointing me toward the city and keeping me on track. I could follow it. As long as I kept to my side, I was assured of an easy passage. The other side of the road was covered in bayou trees and brambles along with banyan trees and their ever-spreading roots.

Out of the corner of my eye, my tree shivered and a portal formed.

"I have what you need." Puca didn't mince words or prance about.

His usual flirting and jovial laughter were lost with the bowl and his son. Even his form was cold. The skin of his chest carried a hue of blue, as did his lips.

I allowed my floating base to slowly come to a stop. "What is the price?" I asked and since I didn't want to seem weak, I turned to face him.

"Magic." He produced a ring with a glowing red stone.

My legs crumpled under me and my knees met the floor. All the bravado in the world wasn't enough to withstand the stone. There was only one stone that glowed red, and that was the King's stone. Now, right in front of me, Puca, the one-time King, held it.

Momma said it was a Fae killer. She was the Fae that delivered it to the King for Jacques.

I stared up at Puca. The words I wanted to say wouldn't come. Pleading wouldn't change the price. I couldn't say no, even if I wanted to.

I was Puca's tool. The sins of my mother had fallen hardest on me. No amount of human emotions could change anything. The human side of me wanted to scream and cry, to rage at the wind, while my hunter's blood roared with the knowledge I was trapped. I was prey, a plaything to a one-time King's whim.

"Is this it?" I gulped back my rage and pushed it into the water under us.

"I am not going to kill you, little one," he remarked. His chest heaved as he sighed. He ran a hand over his black hair. When our eyes met, the reality of what he was going to do hit me full force.

I wasn't going to die, but I'd wish for it.

His eyes turned a fiery red, and his teeth elongated as fur covered his chest and most of his face.

"Brace yourself, hunter! This will hurt a great deal." He slipped the ring on his right hand and pointed it at me.

Magic wakes rushed at me. They were sharp and grinding. Only the pixies carried the ability to grind bone with their mouths. This was magic, and it hit me like the falling cement of the building that crushed momma.

The magic chewed and sucked the dust off my powers away. My face slammed into the hunter's vine, holding us above the water.

A pounding in my chest mimicked the pounding in my head. The stone drew the magic out like sucking on a straw. I watched as my markings slowly disappeared up my arms, then curled back, as if a song had called them home to the place where all magic waited until called upon again, to serve whatever master sang the right song.

My body began to seize and my limbs cracked against the floorboards. I bit down on my tongue, and the taste of blood flooded my senses to join the agony.

Screams echoed across the water.

My screams.

The magic disappeared from sight, and the night darkened. Tears found their way down my temples and into my hairline. And for the first time in my life, I begged, "Please, please make it stop!" I repeated for hours.

All at once, it did.

I curled onto my side and wept like a baby. My clothes were gone, burned away with the magic that helped create them.

"Now, you can face the iron." Puca sat on his haunches next to me. "I left you enough magic to retrieve the bowl and my son, if you can."

I whimpered, like the human I now resembled. He'd taken it. All of it. I was no more Fae than Shea or any of the other kids I took to Fadmor's CB. Fadmor was now a stronger warlock than I was a Fae.

I couldn't look at him. I didn't want to see the pity in his eyes, or the determined set of his shoulders. He believed every price was worth the cost. He believed in the cause.

"You can walk in your daylight, just as Fae's of old. Fulfill your task, and I will restore your station. Fail and…" The sound of his voice faded as he stepped through the portal he'd opened. "I think we both know there is no room for failure, Mercia."

The portal closed. I could barely make out the edges of the opening.

The waking residual magic that was probably floating through the air wasn't there for me to see.

It was gone, all gone. Even the voices of the flittermice. I was alone. I shivered as a cool breeze found its way across the bayou. No longer did magic warm me. Even my hunter's cloak was beyond my grasp.

My floating shack was useless to me. I didn't have the magic to move it.

I sat up and riffled through my bag. There was an old shirt. I slipped it over my head. The shirt belonged to Nick, so it hung well below my knees. I belted my quiver on, adding my daggers, rifle, and bow.

The weight was more than my human frame could carry. I took the gun off and shoved it back in the shack with a lingering glance. The tree would have to hold on to my secrets. At least it was a safe haven in the bayou for the bats. They wouldn't have to range as far for food and shelter.

The chirping in the trees was my only proof they were even still here. Yet, I couldn't see them in the darkness. My eyes were no longer as keen.

I didn't have shoes, pants, food, water, or a plan, and it was a long swim to the nearest dock.

For a moment, I let my tears overwhelm me. They fell like the rain sliding down a windowpane to pool at the edge of my chin. My chest burned with humiliation and the terrible loss of part of who I was.

That piece that shouldn't be taken by anyone.

He's taken it.

He took the part that made me, me and I wanted it back.

I closed my eyes to the dark skies and let my mind roam for a second.

Magic changes you. With every song, you gain more. The mere act of singing gathers the magic to you.

I wiped the tears out of my eyes and sniffed away my runny nose. I slapped either side of my face and sang for Jack. The tune wasn't right. I had to try again. However, I couldn't hit the notes, so the magic never bloomed.

Growling in frustration, I sang for the little crocodiles to come and clean their scales. Alice songs or not, they worked for me, and I was grateful.

A gator popped his head up from the water, and I climbed on his back.

"It's time to stop waiting. Tell the others." I pushed a fresh set of tears from my eyes and squinted at the lights off in the distance.

The reflection on the water was only broken by the outline of thirteen sets of alligator eyes, all focused on the same thing - the city just above the waterline.

CHAPTER 19

SARAH

Puca ripped a portal into the shelf next to us. It opened in a garden. My teeth ground into each other as I stepped through. I waited for the portal to close and turned on him.

"Weren't we just here?" I asked in irritation? My wings flared with the open space and the power of air pushed a heavy breeze into Puca's face.

"They are here," he said no more and didn't need to.

I turned and glanced around the garden. There were stones everywhere, stacked for the walkways and raised beds. They were arched and circled. They bent in fantastic ways to create a visual corkscrew. Some were walls, others precariously balanced on edge at odd angles.

"All of them?" I asked and realized how silly I sounded.

"No. Some are for cover," he remarked and slicked his black hair back.

I waited for the shuffle of his steps or a pivot, but the typical show of dancing Puca put on never came.

His eyes were heavy with sadness and the lack of rest. Dark shadows circled his oculars. The skin around his lips was tight and creased.

He is worried.

It was written all over him.

Whatever Jacques was up to was a real threat. Not just his run of the mill, get rid of the Queen for a new one. Oh no. The 3D chess game had moved to a new level for the first time in thousands of years, and Puca didn't see it coming.

"It isn't safe to move the stones at this time. Once I return the red stone, I will begin bringing them to the location of your choice."

"No. Here is fine. I charge you with their protection." I was being lazy, but I didn't care.

That little voice in the back of my mind was nagging at me. It said I might not be able to protect the stones as well as Puca.

What the fuck have I gotten myself into?

He closed his eyes and pinched the bridge of his nose. The lids snapped open, and he stared me down.

"You are playing the most dangerous of games. I am happy to turn the keeping of the stone over to you, so I may continue my… other activities." A menace lingered around him.

The flowers in the garden closed, and their wakes dimmed. They were trying to hide from what was to come.

Puca was going to lose it with me. His wakes were almost black and shaped like vicious knives.

I raised my hand. "You have kept them safe for how long now? I'm good with you keeping them. Now, go help Nick."

I waved him away in dismissal.

Maybe, if I stroke his ego, he'll chill the fuck out.

However, he didn't go.

"I swore to give you the stones of Danu. I cannot go back on my oath. Sarinha, you know what will happen," he gritted out between teeth.

Ugh!

"Fine! After you save Nick, I will take possession," I groused. "Go see my father for the red stone," I stated and turned to take in the garden. Mom loved flowers.

Though, I'm not sure why.

From over my shoulder, Puca huffed before the sound of a portal opening and closing cut him off.

A smile touched the side of my mouth. I won this round. Sort of.

The garden was awash with stonework. None of them looked special or waked differently from the others. I walked around for an hour to see if I could pick out the fakes from the real ones. But nothing came of it. Other than spotting some plants that could have come out of a Dr. Seuss book and a pixie hiding in a gardenia bush, there was nothing. That gave me the willies.

I was shit out of luck. The stones kept their secrets.

I knew that Puca wasn't lying. He couldn't. Magic was a hard taskmaster, the most unforgiving force I knew of. No creature could stand against it or reverse it without the right song.

The notes of a song danced at the tip of my tongue. All I needed was the right vibration and desire to fulfill my wish. I could rip back the magic holding the stones safe.

If I do, who else might see them?

I would be placing the stones in danger. They hold a power I didn't understand. And therein lay the problem. I didn't understand what they were or what they did.

How could I wield a power I don't understand?

Dumb!

I didn't understand magic when I started. I grew to understand it. Yet, that wouldn't work. Not this time. I didn't have that luxury. The learning curve might kill us all or worse.

Jacques had a plan. All I had to do was figure out what that plan was. Playing catch-up at this level made my head hurt.

Maybe a sheet of paper will help?

Then I could write all the info down and look at it.

I shook my head. A murder board would work better. The vision of Sherlock Holmes smoking a pipe while listening to the violin flashed through my mind.

If smoking a pipe would help, I'd do it.

Jacques wanted the stone circle, a bowl, and a wand.

Internally, I groaned.

God!

It sounded like a spell from one of those faux witchcraft books the stores carried before the Fae came.

The knockoff book of shadows say, '*All you need is a circle and a bowl; get naked under the full moon, and wave your wand around clockwise.*'

Ugh!

Of course, it sounded like a witch's spell because it was. It was magic.

When there was television, all the shows had a eureka moment, where the lead character figured it all out.

That was Arty's favorite part. His reply afterward would always be '*I knew it!*' making me shake my head.

I blinked to clear my eyes. For a moment, Arty stood before me with his glasses looking at me through his eyebrows, trying to hold back a shy smile.

I grabbed a sheet of mental sandpaper and removed that vision.

I never believed that those moments happened, the eureka ones. Since I'd entered the Hallowed Hills, the only time I could equate remotely close to that was figuring out what notes to sing to unlock the doors.

Even that wasn't me figuring it out. I overheard Janice.

My chest clenched.

Those lines of thought had to die. I couldn't go down either of those roads. Janice and Arty needed to get off the train my thoughts were on. I didn't have time for them.

I couldn't let my feelings interfere with my eureka moment. And it was a eureka moment.

I stood in a garden filled with stones that Danu claimed would lead her to another world.

It hit me that her journals were so different and wrong. They weren't journals, not in the traditional sense. They weren't diaries either. The accounts were methodical, to the point of crazy. She'd listed everything she did to activate the stones, like in science class.

A quote kept hopscotching through my mind - any sufficiently advanced technology can look like magic.

It didn't matter who said it. They were dead. Anyone who wanted to complain about me forgetting was dead too. But the words were still true.

There was this movie my mom liked which was called '*The Gods must be crazy*.' It was about an African tribe and how a coke bottle fell from the sky almost ruined their lives, until one guy decided to return it to the Gods.

At the time, I thought it was funny. Well, at least, the first time I watched it. After that, I just thought it was stupid. Now, I could see it for what it really was - a truth I didn't think could be true.

The stones of Danu were no different from that coke bottle. We were not ready for whatever they were, and we couldn't have them. I had to find a way to get rid of them. Hiding them wasn't good enough anymore.

I can't give them back to the Gods since Danu is dead.

This magic spell must never be used. This technology was too great for us.

I sang a fresh layer of protection over the meadow. Puca's shields weren't always that great. After all, I managed to break through one when I was still oh so very human.

I opened a portal. I needed a crash course in Latin, then I needed to read until my eyes bled. Because whatever Danu made was going to get us all killed, and I couldn't let that happen.

Fae depended on me to save them from themselves. I couldn't let them down. They were like my children now. They were like teenagers who you mostly, love but also hate. They do stupid shit, and you have to punish them. Yet, every so often, they surprise you.

Right now, I was surprised, but like any other Mother of their race, I was smarter. Jacques had worked the system for generations, manipulating everything and everyone.

His big downfall was that he thought like a Fae. I needed to start thinking like a Queen.

CHAPTER 20

MERCIA

There was one song that all Fae of every level could use - glamor. The song grew first in my mind, then spread to my belly.

It was the first song I'd tried that didn't feel like swimming through the mud in order to reach the magic. And I needed that magic badly now.

"Thank you, Danu, for leaving even the weakest of Fae a way to hide from wicked eyes." I wet my lips and sat up as straight as my spine would hold me. I pulled a full breath of air into my chest and released the music held there.

"One for sorrow,
Two for joy,
Three for a girl,
Four for a boy,
Five for silver,
Six for gold,
Seven for a Fae secret never to be told."

The magic burst forth, and like a bubble, popped right over my head. I tipped my chin up so I could enjoy the feeling of the spell taking hold. But the feeling wasn't there, only the reality of how weak I was and the lump in my throat that I didn't want.

Damn these witches!

Rage wrapped around me. I ground my teeth. All I could see was Cassidy, Larka, and all the other warlocks and witches that used weaker Fae and humans to their advantage.

The choice I made in front of Fadmor's CB never felt so right as it did now.

I'm weak, but I won't always be.

Plain old humans would be just like those with the thinnest of Fae blood would. They would never reach the level I was. They wouldn't live long enough. Unless they survive a close dance with death.

I looked down at the gator under me. He was a good sort. Older, but wiser, carrying the scars of all the fights he'd won.

My hand went to the phantom scar on my hip. That injury never left a mark only because of Nick.

I could do this. If I did it the right way, everyone could get what they want.

I hummed to reveal the magic like momma taught me. The magic took hold, and I held my breath. It was weak, and I had to hum it three more times to amp the vision up.

It was a waste of time. There was no trail, not for Nick or the witches that took him.

It was a pipe dream to think it would still be there after all this time. It had been weeks, and magic trials didn't last unless you put a tracker on someone.

My nostrils flared.

I slapped both sides of my face to get my blood up as high as my emotions felt. The adrenaline was jet fuel for a mostly human part Fae.

I opened my mouth to sing a Jack song. My jaw snapped closed on the habit. I needed to look as human as possible, and being too light-footed would have looked strange.

I directed the gator to the backside of a building with three stories sticking up out of the water. Iron waked around the base of the structure. My normal response was to cringe away. At this range, I should have felt something. I didn't. There were no welts, no burning, not even the warmth of a fire. I heaved a sigh of relief and slipped off the side of the gator.

"Tell your friends to keep an eye out. I'm going in. If you need to reach me, send a gator. I can't hear the flittermice anymore."

The gator snapped his jaw open and closed three times in understanding. I ran a hand down the leathery skin between his eyes until I reached a nostril. He huffed and sprayed water at me, then turned and swam away. His body shifted back and forth with only the dawning light glimmering off his exposed body.

I dove under the water and swam into one of the open underwater windows.

My barefoot kicked something, and it burned me. I cried out, and the murky water rushed in. My hands clawed at the water dragging me up to an air pocket near the ceiling of the room. I didn't want to whimper, so I bit my lip.

It was iron.

It could burn me, but only on contact. I worked to slow my breathing, using the exercise to push my memories of Cassidy's iron box back into the past.

My breathing became rhythmic, and even, so I ducked back under, searching for a way up to the next floor.

The stairs were wide and still intact. I would be surprised, but the wood was spelled.

The magic reminded me of Fadmor and his CB doors. This spell wasn't layered. It was old, twenty years at least.

It didn't matter. I wasn't Fae enough for it to stop me.

Maybe Puca wasn't such an asshole. If I was more Fae at this point, I'd have never made it this far that fast. Babysitting a changeling wasn't really my flavor, anyway.

I snorted at my cup half-full tale. It was bullshit. I didn't want this, but an advantage was an advantage. Everything was a weapon.

My iron-burned foot touched the wooden stair, and I tiptoed up to the landing.

I wished I could pull my hunter cloak. That magic was just out of reach. I kept to the shadows anyway out of habit. Even without a Jack song, I was light on my feet.

I hummed under my breath the cleaning song, drying my long shirt and leaving no doubt that I hadn't come out of the water.

I moved into the hall.

My face fell slack, and my eyes took on the vacant stare of the entranced. My steps turned even and steady. I slowly turned the door handle and stepped out onto the raised walkways of New Orleans.

So far, so good.

I joined the flow of morning humans going about their chores. I did my best to keep my eyes from moving too much and held my head still.

My heartbeat was in my ears, and it sounded more like a drum, then the stout heart of a killer and savior.

I'd never thought of myself as a savior, but I was. I'd saved Shea and the rest of the kids.

Everyone but Ron.

After this it was Ron's turn. I wouldn't leave anyone behind, not again.

I walked for an hour past buildings and cats, lots of cats. The orange calicos couldn't see through my glamor. They were the wrong kind of cat.

The black ones were another story. I avoided them as much as I could. They were like the underbosses of a CB. They reported to the black cat with yellow eyes, the one I desperately hoped I wouldn't see.

I finally began to recognize one of the waterways when I spotted the black cat with yellow eyes.

He was sitting on a dock, cleaning a paw and whipping it over an ear when one of the calicos sauntered up and rubbed against him. He yowled at the girly cat. Clearly, he didn't like the affection. The calico cringed away. While he was distracted, I took the next turn to skirt the backside of the building before trying to pick up the remembered trail.

But my luck ran out. There, sitting smack dab in the middle of my path, was a black cat with green eyes. He saw me, and I saw him.

Before he could open his mouth to send up the alarm, I tossed a finger dagger and lodged it in his chest, pinning him to the wooden walkway.

Old habits die hard, and I hummed as I took off down the walkway. The return-to-me song worked, and my finger dagger snapped to my hand.

A fresh round of adrenaline flooded my system. I sang for Jack and to make me nimble, and the spell fell flat. I didn't have time to think about how that would affect the outcome of my mad dash.

Instead, I took the next turn and hopped from one raised deck to another. I slipped into a building and quickly made my way through a room.

As I was about to step out onto the next dock, I stopped short. The door to a closet stood open, revealing women's clothes.

I glanced down at my attire and went back to the closet. I shoved the finger dagger back into my belt and stepped into the large dressing room.

Most of the clothes were various shades of black and gray, just like the witches at the cave.

Internally I groaned. They were the old kind of witches.

Ugh! Don't they get it?

I shook my head. Momma said that before the fall, witches believed black gave them power. They wore it to show the world like a badge. It didn't make sense to me. Why black?

Magic comes from nature and song, not from color.

I shook my head.

At least, I would be able to spot them on the walkways.

I pushed the black clothes to the side and pulled out a ragged pair of pants, slipping them on under my droopy shirt. I'd just gotten them cinched up when someone came in.

"Did you see him? So good-looking. I hope they choose me for the main breeding program." The woman sounded young and excited.

"They may choose more than usual for this stud. Did you see his eyes? The prettiest green I've ever seen. Can you imagine what his children will look like?" The woman was practically drooling.

There was only one male I knew with eyes that green.

Nick!

They must have seen him. Part of me wanted to rip their throats out for thinking he would breed with them. My hunter blood wanted to kill them where they stood.

Nick is mine.

Instead, I let the rush pass. My human side made it easier than before.

Just one more reason to be thankful to Puca.

Not that I was ever going to say that to him.

Yuck! Thanks are for humans.

The most human thing I'd ever said was *'sorry'* and that was only because Cassidy forced me. That would never happen again.

A *'thank you'* was number two on the list of shit Fae never said.

I snuggled back into the shadows of the closet and pulled a fresh brown shirt down from a shelf. I removed my belt, slipping my weapons to the floor, then pulled the brown shirt over the one I already wore.

I reattached my weapons and sat down to wait for the horny mutts in the next room to leave.

It was well into the afternoon when they finally left. I almost fell asleep from listening to their drivel. They twittered about the most mundane bullshit in the world.

The truth was I'd rather have had a duel with a kelpie with one arm behind my back than listen to one more minute of those two bloated windbags yammering.

However, they did impart more intel than one would think. Even better, I knew enough about them to pull a glamor. The younger witch was about my size. Doing her would require a double glamor, one for looks, the other for sound. But I could do it.

With every song I sang, my power grew. I just needed to stay weak long enough to get out of here alive. At this rate, I'd be strong enough to call for Jack, and then I'd be cooking with some real grease.

Rather than use my witchy glamor, I tucked that into my back pocket.

I'd save that for a real need - the backup plan/exit plan. *It can work for both.*

I mentally shrugged and double-checked the glamor I was already wearing. I turned to the mirror in the closet to check my look.

The tips of my hair was white. Other than that, I looked like any other Fae-zombified human. I sang a fresh round of glamor to change my hair, making it look normal. Then, I stepped out onto the platform and moved into the flow of foot traffic.

I surveyed the area for cats and noted how many witches were out and about. Now that I knew what to look for, spotting my enemies was easy. They were all dressed in black.

My hands itched to plant a blade deep in the chest of every black-clad torso I came across. The human side won over the Fae hunter.

I kept my hand loose at my sides and continued my recon, mentally mapping the city.

CHAPTER 21

Sarah

The edge of the purple war forest was lined with wilted mushrooms. They lay on their sides and atop of each other. Some still held their form.

I glanced around at the forest floor to pick out the weapons littered there. Other than my gun and silver, I didn't carry another weapon. But it was comforting to know there was more about it if I needed one.

The forest was massive, and from where I stood, there was no sign of Jacques or Finian.

Rather than wait for them to appear, I sang. I didn't need the entire song, only the chorus.

"Georgie Porgy,

Pudding, and pie

Kissed poor Fae and made them cry.

When my other children came out to play,

Georgie Porgy ran away."

I pictured Georgie as Jacques and let the magic do its work.

All the Fae in the Hallowed Hills that were sworn to me began to arrive. The surrounding air swelled with power. Each Fae carried its own tune or resonance.

Just as Danu said.

Her books were enlightening. Jacques only won the battle the last time because he managed to divide Fae along the lines of the two courts.

My little display of bloodlust in the throne room made it clear I would cut down anyone in my path.

I am no Danu.

I didn't create Fae. They weren't my babies. Yet, I adopted them, so they were my children.

This wasn't a democracy. It was a despotism and I had absolute power. Jacques would bend to me or die along with everyone who sides with him. Then, I would make new Fae, to replace them.

Because only I have that power.

"You have called us all to the battlefield. What now?" Cernunnos asked as his baritone rumbled the surrounding air.

Because he died in the eyes of magic, he wasn't able to retain any of his King's power. Not like Puca.

Puca was released. Jillian made a grave mistake when she let him go free. I made the same mistake when I chose to entrap Deston and Jacques rather than kill them.

That won't happen again.

"I want this forest scoured and every Fae not sworn to me, cut down. I don't have time for anyone who betrays their Queen or Fae." I didn't raise my voice, but the silence of the valley carried it to the very edges.

The body of the crowd spread out into the remains of the purple forest, keeping in sight of one another. Humanity used to use the same tactics to search large areas.

The high ground was where I stayed. There was no reason for me to leave it. When my sworn army moved beyond the site, I took to my wings and hovered over the ancient battlefield watching.

That was something Danu hadn't done. The records showed her on a horse during the battle. She didn't take to the sky and kill her first-born son — Jacques.

She should have.

We would all be living very different lives if she had only steeled herself and done what needed doing.

One life for the thousands that fell on this field. The needs of the many against the needs of the few.

How did she let the few win out?

I shook my head since musing wasn't the answer.

On the edge of the forest, I spied Mod. She was hovering on a round.

In one swift motion of my wings, I was headed toward her. She lowered her round to the valley floor and kneeled.

"My Queen," she murmured with downcast eyes. Her left arm crossed over her chest along with her fingers. She tipped her head up and touched her forehead.

I wasn't in the mood for small talk, so I didn't bother to speak at all.

Mod took to her feet and began, "Jacques left much in his castle. Apparently, Pil opened his most secret of secrets before she fled to the surface - his personal chambers."

My mouth must have hung open because the moisture on my tongue disappeared.

"You don't say," I replied.

Perhaps Pil really had changed sides or maybe she never was on Jacques' side.

"Jacques doesn't know that it was her. I spread word that she was on the surface. Just to throw him off," she informed me with a smug smile.

"Did it ever occur to you that I didn't want him to know where she was?" I asked irked. "As long as he thinks Pil was down here, he would be too," I hissed.

Mod dropped to the ground unconcerned with whatever dirt and grim was there. "I… I… I will make it right, my Queen."

Her stuttering was noticeable enough for me to forgive her.

She is on my side, or so I think.

Now Jacques would try to find a way to the surface. He would expect Pil to help him.

"Did you find anything useful?" I asked.

She droned on about tapestries and holes in tables. None of which mattered.

I was only half listening. I waved her on toward the rest of my army to keep searching the forest remains.

Pil was dead, and Jacques didn't know. There were only three people in the Hallowed Hills that did, other than me.

Puca never told anyone anything. Alice didn't even know Jacques was free, and Nick was on the surface. I swallowed.

Nick was in trouble. Jacques was looking for Pil. He didn't know about Mercia. But tracking a changeling on the surface with her level of Fae blood should be a pretty easy job.

The image in my mind petrified me - Mercia.

Nick is keeping watch over her and Jacques will find her.

My teeth clamped down on the lip I didn't realize I was biting. The coppery taste of blood flooded into my mouth, and I used it to swallow back my fear.

Nick!

Jacques would use him to get to me and Puca.

Before another thought could form, my bloody lips were whistling for Puca. This was twice in one day, and I hated myself for it. Puca would do his dance to get what he wants.

I tilted my head back and squeezed my eyes shut. As the sound of magic ripping a portal open broke the silence of the valley, I opened my eyes to face him.

"Sarinha." The scent of leather and horse followed Puca, announcing his presence wherever he went better than a bell.

How to ask for what I want?

It was the Fae way - to play the word games and dance an innuendos edge. Every conversation was a double-edged sword. Each statement was a coming and going of verbs and nouns. The definitions spun out to the third degree and the obscure.

I pulled a heavy breath of air through my nose and began. "Nick, where is he?" It was the most innocuous question I could muster without revealing myself too much.

"New Orleans," Puca whispered over my shoulder. He wasn't trying to compel or tease me. He just annoied me.

"Why in the ever Lovin hell would he go there?" I demanded.

I should have held back.

There were a thousand other things I could've said and didn't.

"He was captured." He put up his hand to quiet me, "No need to worry yourself. I have the problem well in hand," Puca remarked.

The tired crinkles around his eyes were gone. He'd only been gone for twenty minutes tops. But that translated to days on the surface.

Perhaps he took a nap.

"Jacques knows Pil went to the surface," I offered.

I didn't know if Puca would reach the same conclusions I did.

"It isn't a problem. He won't find her because she's dead," Puca shrugged and shuffled.

An image flashed before me from my childhood of Madi Grau. I'd watched videos of the Fat-Tuesday parades in New Orleans - all the beads, streamers, confetti, and drinking and…

"What do you mean you have it in hand? New Orleans is covered in iron!" I shouted. The sound hit the leftover trees from the forest and bounced back.

"Mercia will take care of it," he replied, yet the reassurance didn't hit the mark with me.

I shook my head. "No, she won't. That child will leave him to die. No! You can't trust her. She is just like her mother, a killer." I'd grabbed one of Puca's arms to stop him from dancing in a circle around me. Then I shook him.

His teeth grew at an alarming speed, and his lips drew back in a snarl. "You may be Queen, but you don't rule me. Mercia will save Nick. Rest assured."

"WTF makes you think so?" I screamed as my body was shaking.

Nick wasn't just my friend. He was like a brother to me. I couldn't trust his safety to that changeling hunter. I didn't care if she was Arty's child. She was more Pil than Arty.

"Because, granddaughter, she is in love with Nicolas. She will do all in her power to save him, no matter the cost. Now, are you reassured?" He yanked his arm from my grasp and slicked his hair back.

I stepped back, mollified.

"What if Jacques reaches her and turns her to get to us?" The daisy chain of possible events played out like a game of hopscotch in my mind.

"He can't turn what is mine." He threw a simpering smile at me and opened a portal. "Now, if there isn't anything else, I have things to do."

He leaped through the opening then blew me a kiss before letting it close.

"Yeah, but he can torture it," I murmured under my breath.

Can't turn what is mine.

I yammered to myself. He really did think a great deal of himself.

His.

She was sworn to him. That was the only reason he was so smug.

Ugh!

I ground down on my teeth.

"We've finished, my Queen. The forest is empty. Jacques was here for a short period of time."

I turned to face Cernunnos who paced like an animal.

"I can track him if you let me," he growled. The light in his eyes told me he was hungry for the hunt.

All I could see was the purple of the forest mushroom. They laid everywhere on the ground.

My father never ceased pacing. My army reassembled nearby, and I hummed a protective skin. They were sworn to me, but trust is earned, and there wasn't one person here who had earned it.

"Were there any signs of Janice?"

Cernunnos moved to my side. "His trail was here, but it was subdued. He's being held in some magical fashion," he offered.

"Track them! I want to know every blade of grass they step on and every flower they pass," I replied.

Cernunnos stepped away from me and faced the mass of marked faces. Each carried its own colorings and swirls, all the sight of angels.

They took my breath away with their beauty. The mass wasn't just from the Seelie court. There were UnSeelie too. The entire seasonal divides were here.

The yuletide Fae with their white hair and blue-tinged skin lingered beside the summer tans. Autumn carried more henna-colored marking while spring was a riot of bright florals and neons.

I glanced down at my own green marking. No matter how much I thought this wasn't where I wanted, or should be, it wasn't true. I was always going to be here.

The baritone of the one-time King rumbled through the trees and pounded in hearts.

"We will track this thief and take back the Queen's consort. I need fifty warriors."

I heaved a sigh of thanks. I didn't need to ask. I couldn't. I promised Fae would be different. Yeah, they swore fealty to me, but Jacques would kill anyone in his way.

I will too.

I couldn't ask anyone here to go to their death. They couldn't say no to me. Cernunnos asking gave them a chance to leave and go home.

I learned enough from Danu's journals. She ruled with love and not an iron hand. Every Queen since her had followed Jillian's example - the absolute power of the Queen must not be questioned.

To my utter surprise, more than fifty came forward. They were armed and ready for a long hunt.

Cernunnos came and kneeled at my feet. "My Queen, will you give us your blessing to kill the King?"

Without a moment's hesitation I replied, "Yes, bring me his head." I looked up at the mass before me. "Cut Finian into four pieces and stick them on a pike in the four seasons. I swear by the river Afron, I want all of Fae to see that when you break faith with me, you break faith with all Fae!" I shouted. "You are either with us, or you are our enemy."

The crowd erupted in cheers. There was no love lost here for Jacques.

Cernunnos took to his feet and waved his band to follow. Mod was among them. She nodded her head and crossed her arm over her chest as she passed.

Jacques had minions watching. This was the image they would share with Jacques, making him believe that I was just like all the other Queens.

I. Am. Not.

Rather than dispersing, the mass of Fae followed me back to the castle. I gave them their leave. Yet, none left.

The main corridors held Fae of every flavor. A lone Fomorian stood in the center of the great doorway. The heavy muscles covering his large frame flexed. Fomorians didn't have the use of magic. I wasn't afraid. However, the barely contained strength in their bodies demanded respect.

I crossed my arm over my chest then crossed my fingers before lowering my arm.

He returned my acknowledgement, and he wasn't the only one. But he was the first I'd seen since I sat on the stone throne.

"Me come to serve! Me protect the Queen." The Fomorian used his one arm to slap his chest. The sound gathered the attention it was intended to.

I tilted my head.

His thick lips pulled back into a smile dotted by the missing teeth. He didn't enter the castle properly. Instead, he took up guard to one side of the door, then he grunted at one of his brothers and used his arm to push him to the other side.

He patted his hand at the ground to indicate *stay*. His burgundy-colored brother huffed and stopped doing anything other than rolling his single shoulder.

A breeze moved through the opening and I covered my nose to keep the stench at bay. I forgot how much they smelled.

"My Queen, where shall we put them all?" One of the staff asked.

I hummed a few bars of a Crowded House song to reinforce the structure.

"I guess you better clean a few more rooms," I shrugged.

The male bowed and backed away.

Whipping my head back and forth, I took in the crowd, then headed to the library. Lavender, and mom had to have found something.

CHAPTER 22

MERCIA

The sun lowered in the sky, and the bayou grew unbearably hot. I'd not paid attention to the seasons for many years. The hot and cold didn't affect me. My clothes had stayed the same for years.

It should have been a tip-off to Cassidy. It wasn't. It was just another way he'd been tricked. Cassidy, too, didn't change his clothing based on the weather.

Momma only changed based on the terrain and only with magic.

If you didn't understand that warlocks and witches were Fae. I supposed it wouldn't be noticed.

Now with me so close to my humanity, I was dying in the heat. The humidity coated my skin. The stench of the bayou came with it, that scent of slowly decaying plant life mixed with dead fish and trash.

The witches could have called the water to move and carry the rot away, couldn't they? Well, it was the least they could do.

The rest of the zombie humans didn't notice the heat. They were sweating, but they didn't wipe it away.

The itching at the base of my neck returned. Glamors always made me itch. It was my tell. It was the one I'd had to fight my whole life.

Momma paced and I itched. Maybe it was that human part of me I'd like to deny. Arthur, to me, was just a person, the human half of my DNA. I didn't even know what he looked like.

Momma said looks mean nothing. It was the strength of one's song and the wit of one's mind that mattered.

Arthur made her laugh. On the surface, humans laugh all the time. Momma never laughed. Not for real. So, if Arthur made her laugh, he had wit indeed. That alone was reason to admire my sire.

The heat sank into my skin slowly, cooking me like a frog. I couldn't reveal my discomfort. I couldn't sing to cool my skin. That only left me with my wit.

My eyes snagged on the cats. Those familiars were the workhorses of New Orleans. They rubbed on the legs of each and every human. It was a herding technique.

The calicos moved a few humans into each building. If the building was more than one floor above the waterline, they moved more.

The black cats swiped at the stragglers.

A deep male scream issued from a dock on the other side of the waterway. Black cats swarmed over a man desperate to cover his face. The cats clawed at his clothes and skin until he was bleeding.

"What is all this?" A black-clad warlock asked.

The human was lying on his side, whimpering, his arm wrapped around his head, protecting his face.

I moved into the shadows. I hummed for my hunter's cloak. It never came.

"Are you the intruder that killed Mr. Framkins?" The man asked, then kicked the cowering human in the belly.

"I didn't kill anyone," the human mourned.

"It was a cat, you fool. Mr. Framkins was a black cat. You know what the punishment for entering our city and killing a pet is, don't you?" The warlock kicked the human again, this time in the lower back.

I moved out of the shadowy alcove and began walking. My pace was set as slow as I dared. They were looking for me. If they even knew it was me.

"I'm only here for my son. I just want him back." That human was out of his mind.

They weren't going to return his son, not ever.

This city was the death place of anyone less than a touch of Fae. Even that might not save you.

The warlock squatted, "If you want to be with him so badly, why didn't you say so?" His voice was low and deceptively soft. "We aren't Fae. You can join him in service to the New Orleans coven." The warlock petted the human's hair back.

The human whimpered.

I wanted to shake my head. I knew what was coming. That human should have packed up what he had left and sought refuge with the nearest witch or warlock. He never should have come here.

Warlocks liked to toy more with their playthings. They liked examples.

He laced his fingers into the man's hair and yanked his head back at a painful angle.

The human sniffled. His face was covered in scratches and blood. Part of his nose was missing. The scent of ammonia, fear, well piss really, drifted over the water.

I flared my nostrils and fought the scowl that kept trying to take over my face.

This didn't need to happen. That warlock didn't need to scare the shit out of the guy.

Pixies shit! Just get on with it!

The cruelty of it was what got to me. I didn't like to play with my prey. I liked the thrill of the hunt and the kill. This was plain wicked.

Was that why momma didn't want me to come here?

The warlock took out a knife and cut the rest of the man's nose off. The screaming rang across the water.

Part of me wanted to run. That part of my psyche was more human. On the other hand, the Fae hunter wanted to start a new hunt with the warlock as my quarry.

The warlock licked the piece of flesh and inspected his trophy before slipping it into the folds of his jacket.

The human was still screaming. A pride of black cats all sat patiently in a circle, watching the scene unfold. The warlock sang the enchantment song and the human's screams were cut off. His eyes milked over, and he took to his feet.

Blood dripped from the wound in the middle of his face. It followed along his lip line then worked its way into the space between his upper and lower lips.

He licked some of it away. The rest of the blood ran down his chin to drip off onto his shirt.

The warlock snickered to himself and dusted off the shoulders of the human as if the blood wasn't causing a mess.

"Tell me again, why did you kill Mr. Framkins?" The sweet cadence of the warlock was pathetic. I supposed he fancied himself a master villain.

"Didn't kill Mr. Framkins," the human replied in a dull voice.

The warlock whirled around to face the pride of cats. "There's another one. Find them!"

He sang for a boat and pushed it into the waterway, heading to one of the raised graveyards.

I hummed under my breath, hoping the hunter's tracking spell would take, then sighed in relief when it did.

It was weak and wouldn't last long. I picked up my pace while keeping the zombie effect believable.

The warlock still managed to pull away. Crossing raised walkways and hopping from one dock to another, I reached the end of the line.

From behind, a cat yowled and hissed. I froze. The cat swiped at my leg, urging me to follow him. I turned to find not one, but six cats sitting in the middle was the yellow-eyed cat. All the hair covering his back reached for the sky while his tail resembled the electrical charge of a lightning storm.

The low growl that issued from the group told me I was in for a hell of a time. I did the only thing I could - I turned and jumped into the water.

Part of me had hoped to find the water refreshing. It was lukewarm. I moved my arms, pushing as much as I could with only a human's abilities.

The sound of yowling and hissing receded into the background, only to be replaced by the slapping of wood on water. I turned enough to get a glimpse of a boat heading my way. I had two choices: turn and fight or dive and hope to outwit them.

I chose option three.

I sang Alice's gator song and watched as the three moved the boat into the swamp. The clicking sound of snapping jaws and screams of pain worked to cover my next song.

I called for Jack to be nimble and the magic took and settled over me. The layering of the spell worked to quicken my speed as I swam away.

Water wasn't my best fighting field. I never noticed the other boat until they were pulling me out of the water. One had a hold of my hair, the other my belt.

"Now, I think this is the one. She killed Mr. Framkins," the male warlock laughed as he shook me by my hair. My glamor held enough to hide my weapons. My eyes and hair were lost to the Jack song.

I stared at the two warlocks and blinked as their wake lines flashed in and out.

"There's something wrong with her eyes," the second warlock remarked.

The first warlock shook my head again. "The only thing wrong with her eyes is that they aren't enchanted. This one killed a pet." He stared down at my face and sneered. "You know what we do to killers, don't you?"

I didn't want to give too much away, so I whined, "No."

"Torne, she doesn't know. Should we tell her or let her find out on her own?"

Torne smiled, "Witches like to experiment. Don't they, Kane?"

Kane, the first warlock, laid a big wet kiss on my lips. "That's a kiss goodbye. Once you enter the tunnels, no one will ever see you again."

They didn't think I was a witch. There was no fear of reprisals here.

Tunnels aren't usually easy to get out of. With Nick, that wouldn't be a problem. The magic would understand why I needed Nick.

"Is that where you take your breeding stock?" I asked.

Kane slapped the side of my head.

"We aren't going to breed with a mutt like you. Why? Did you like that kiss?" his lips worked over mine again. I kissed him back, thrusting my tongue down his throat.

By Danu, I hate minions!

They always did the same shit.

Momma said sex was a weapon. I'd left it in my arsenal for too long. But it was time to use everything I had.

I gulped back my thoughts of Nick and embraced the warlock before me.

I worked my lips over his, and he pulled me into his lap. His hands dug into my ass. It seemed like it was going to work. He whispered words in my ear that I didn't bother to listen to and touched everything.

Even Cassidy had never touched me like this. Bile climbed my throat. I swallowed it back. He bit my neck, and then Torne joined in, by sliding his hand between my thighs and rubbing his fingers into Kane's.

Oops!

"She told me, not you. Get your own!" Kane growled.

I glanced over my shoulder. If Torne really got into it, he would notice the bow across my back. That would be a problem.

"She's going to the tunnels anyway. What do you care if I take a piece?" Torne retorted.

Kane stood up, and I slid down with a plop onto the floorboards. I was about to sing for the gators when Kane pushed Torne over the side. The last thing I saw out of the corner of my eye as my head slammed into the edge of the boat.

———

My eyes opened and closed. The flash of the yellow birds of Fae flying around my face disappeared. The pain of the impact didn't.

"She may never wake up. Why bother with any treatments if she can't perform?" a young man asked.

I closed my eyes and let my face go slack.

"Look, we give her a treatment and wait. If she doesn't wake up in a day or two, we give her a shot of adrenaline straight to the heart and see what happens," a woman replied.

"That could burst her heart. You have no idea what health history she has."

"And I don't care. We have a Fae, we know what the Govs are up to, and I'm not going to blow this chance. If we can make an army, we can run everything," she retorted.

Greed God! It never goes away!

These mutts were as greedy as any Fae. I wanted to shake my head at the stupidity of it all.

Changeling or full Fae, human, or halfbreed, they all wanted more. None of them were happy with what they had. The only guy I knew that didn't want more was Fadmor.

I mentally snickered at my rhyme.

"I don't understand why we don't just stick to the breeding program?" The guy was upset.

"Because that Fae won't breed—" the woman huffed.

I must have made a sound because they both stopped talking.

"Prep her. I want the operation done today," the woman said.

She pried my eyes open. "Good morning. How do you feel?" She asked.

I blinked, then retched my head away from her hands without responding.

"Can you speak?"

I turned and caught a glimpse of the guy leaving the room. He was a little older than me in human time. I appeared to be twenty years old.

She patted my cheek as if there was something wrong with my mind. "Can you speak? Don't worry about the other

Doctor. He's only here to assist me. I'm Dr. Chock." She smiled down at me.

I pressed my lips flat to keep all the questions in.

"Well, guess that answers that, doesn't it? You don't want to talk to me? That's okay. You don't need to right now."

She moved around the table, testing the straps holding me down. "I hope you don't mind we took all your clothes off. We need you as clean as possible, and your clothes were dirty." She ran her hands over my body.

"This is very exciting," she laughed.

I was covered in a light cotton fabric. It was so clean I could almost believe it was cleaned by fairies. The loose dress reached my thighs. There were socks on my feet and wrapped around them, restraints.

The table was plain stainless steel metal, with no hint of iron.

"I haven't decided if we should put you under or keep you awake for the procedure."

I zoomed in on her and the word she'd just used.

"Oh, you understand what I'm talking about?" She laughed.

The last time I'd heard that word was in the tower in Portland, near my old CB. The woman there called what she was doing a procedure.

"What procedure?" I asked.

"Awe, you can talk. Good." She petted my hair back from my face. "I'm going to first irradiate your body, then I'm going to implant someone else's bone marrow into you." She tapped my nose as if I was a human child.

My heart hammered out of my chest. I closed my eyes. I didn't want to give myself away.

"So you know what I'm talking about? Good. Ethically, I should explain everything to you. That is the Hippocratic oath. But everything we do down here is unethical. So there is no point," Dr. Chock sighed.

My fingers curled into a fist, and I yanked on the restraints holding my arms to my side, and kicked my feet. Tears formed to blur my vision.

There would be no one this time to save me. Nick was there, somewhere just as trapped as me.

I screamed as I pulled and yanked. It didn't change one thing. I was Fae-fucked. The only person who could reach me was Puca and he would never come.

He expected me to complete the mission.

I've already failed once.

Dr. Chock pressed my shoulders back onto the cold metal table. "I know you are a plain old human. If you survive, you will be able to use magic. Just like us." She smiled brightly as if that was every human's dream. "Won't that be great?" she blinked with her fake smile.

As if imparting magic makes it all okay.

"What if I don't want to be like you?" I grit out. I knew that I should have shown more fear, maybe cry like a weak baby.

These tears of anger can be used to my advantage.

Yet, I couldn't.

Why did every changeling do shit like this? All of them but me. I didn't hate humans or Fae, Even though I thought I did at one time.

The truth hit me hard - Puca freed me of that. I chose to help humanity rather than reject my human side. Puca made me choose.

However, I rejected this part of humanity. These witches weren't human. They were pure UnSeelie and evil. This could not be allowed to survive.

The sting of a needle-breaking skin pinched at the inside of my elbow. Dr. Chock taped the butterfly-shaped handle down.

The needle was attached to a little tube that led to a bag swinging from a metal hook. It all looked just like that OR room in the tower.

I whistle for Nick and squeeze my eyes closed. Nothing happened.

Panic moved through me. My breath quickened, and my pulse jumped as my heart turned over in my chest. I frantically glanced down at my hip, searching for the blood I expected to see there.

Hysteria was rising, and I couldn't stop it.

"I'll kill you!" I shout.

I was thrashing uncontrollably. They were going to cut me into little pieces and spread me around to make their magic stronger.

"No! Don't cut me up." I cried.

I pressed my lips together to whistle, but the tune was off. I couldn't call for Puca. He wasn't coming. A burning started in my eyes and moved down my face and into my chest, lodging itself there.

"Stop! You'll injure yourself," the doctor said and then called to the guy, "Get me 3 CC's of Demerol. She's hysterical."

"I'm going to hunt you to the ends of the Earth!" I screamed.

I couldn't stop. I wanted to fight. I hummed, but the magic didn't take. I couldn't make a good tune and the notes drifted away.

I called for the gators. Nothing. My throat was sore. "If you do this, I will become your worst nightmare. You wait. I will be the scourge of New Orleans." I was screaming randomly now, grasping for anything I could verbally throw at her. I wanted to scare her.

"You shouldn't have told her." The kid chided as he slipped a needle into a little port near my arm.

"I'll kill you all." Momma's mantra rolled off my tongue as the drug moved through my system. "I'm a hunter." My eyes grew heavy. "I never give up." Each word came out weaker than the one before. "I am the predator. All else is prey." *Prey* was barely a whisper.

CHAPTER 23

SARAH

I never reached the library. Not that anyone in the castle needed to know that. Instead, I flew to the top of the stairway to heaven and exited the structure via a window in one of the towers. Before I could reach the outskirts of the castle gardens, I was bracketed by rounds carrying Fomorians. They hummed to maneuver. Other than that, there were no words spoken.

The lack of communication was a relief. I didn't want to talk. I was all talked out.

The wind of Fae pushed my hair back, and the power of my wings beat my frustration away.

I moved over the remains of the purple forest to pick up Jacques' trail. My father's was there too. He had a head start and more practice.

I didn't think that was going to be a problem. I was a quick study, and, well, I liked to win.

I raced around the four seasons of the Hallowed Hills until my wings burned with the exertion. I wanted this to end. I wanted to sleep and feel safe. Truth be told, what I really wanted I could never have.

Puca told me to let Mercia save Nick, to focus on the larger threat — Jacques.

The trail split and the shine of Jacques headed off into the edges of Fae where Wyld ruled full time. Cernunnos and his band followed that magical trail. Yet, the trail before me forked in a very distinctive pattern. The silver of Jacques' magic went both ways.

"Queen?" The lead Fomorian asked. His rudimentary use of language didn't interrupt my line of thought or irritate me. He had no agenda.

"Can you see a magic trail?"

"No. That not for us. We not use magic well." The others grunted in agreement.

"If a trail divides, what would you think?"

Maybe, if I talk it out, I can make a choice.

"Magic no be in two places." He rolled his shoulder, then picked his nose and flicked it on his round.

I bit my lip. "Yeah, that's what I thought," I said to myself.

No one can be in two places at once.

I turned to the nearest Fomorian, "What's over there?" I asked, waving a hand in the opposite direction from the trail Cernunnos followed.

He grunted, "Lava cave."

The hunt sang in my blood, pulling me to track Jacques and kill him. I swallowed back that desire. I closed my eyes and heaved a deep sigh.

I had to trust that Cernunnos would succeed on his end. He was the better hunter. Just like I had to trust Mercia would save Nick. I quivered just thinking about that.

They were both parts of the bigger picture. Their fights were skirmishes. I had to fight the war.

I knew that I couldn't fight on every front and hope to win every battle.

War doesn't work like that.

Daddy told me you had different portions of the service because they did different jobs.

The army was for a ground war, for Earth. Air-force to dominate the skies, air, navy for aquatic control, water, and so on. Within each group, there were highly specialized people. They were trained to fight at the highest levels.

That was the human army. They were missing an element.

Fire.

That was the one challenge I missed during the Wyld hunt. Even though Ignis gave me the power to wield fire, I didn't earn it. That was part of Fae, a part I'd never faced or embraced.

Jacques was fighting for all the marbles, and I was fighting for the Fae. I wasn't meeting him on the battlefield with everything.

Someone went to face the fire. I should have expected I would need to as well.

"Lead the way!" I ordered.

The mahogany-colored Fomorians moved in closer while one took the lead. We headed away from one trail to investigate another.

I didn't know what color to expect, red, orange, green, or blue.

Fire comes in many forms?

The cave was lined in crystals. They varied in colors from the white of quartz to the deep black of obsidian, each carrying their particular vibrational tone. The wakes in the room collided with one another, only to create a new sound. All of this was just something that you passed through on your way to the big show.

Beyond these crystals was a glow that hummed in the background. It flickered with the power of fire. The flame of elemental control worked over the cavern, beating like a heart into your form.

Heat was the first thing I noticed. The crystal formations lining the walls hung down or jutted out to greet you on the verge of melting. They dripped with mineral-infused liquid. That was how intense the heat was.

And like the human body, it worked to engulf you. The furnace of the human heart pumped not only life, but also heat. It warmed you or cooked you to death.

This cave was the heart of a world, either fueling or stewing it into something else. The tunnel closed in on me, forcing me to touch down and walk.

I flashed to visual weight points in the tunnel. Depth perception was easily distorted by the radiating heat. Slowing down for safety wasn't in my plan. I didn't think we had time.

The silver magic trail was melting away in the heat, and I couldn't chance losing it.

Eventually, the tunnel opened, revealing a cathedral-sized cavern with a river of lava at my feet. On the ground lay a dagger. The handle was plain and practical. Typically, Fae carried ornate, pretty tools and weapons. This was a weapon for war - deadly with no emotional attachment to worry over. It belonged to a warrior.

Janice!

The vetiver and spice scent still lingered on the hilt. I clutched it to my chest.

I allowed a moment of time to stand still, a moment to drink in my worry over Janice and his safety. But that moment passed in a flash.

Fae is watching. Always.

My wings found the air light and turbulent. The churning of the liquid rock bubbled and popped, sending burning ore in every direction.

The splatter hit like the hot oil from a deep fryer. I moved deeper into the cave, searching for Jacques.

The magic trail was jumbled, the heat mixing it and swirling with the wakes being given off.

I moved from one dry rocky outcropping to another.

Janice had to be awake to leave his dagger.

It had to be a crumb for me or anyone I sent to follow. He had to know I would follow him, that Jacques would be on my most wanted list with or without Janice.

The cave opened into new underground rooms to cook your mind and burn your skin. Bits of liquid rock landed on my legs, peppering me with burn marks. I could sing for a protection bubble and save myself from the pain.

It didn't matter. The pain kept me focused. The pressure in my chest couldn't take over if I had something else to think about.

Finally, the cave came to an end. The trail led nowhere.

I turned to face my sentinels and growled. The sound echoed, colliding with the fire wakes.

I landed on a cliff to pace. There had to be a way out of this cave. The trail had to show me where they went.

A bubble formed on the lake of lava and grew. It burst to reveal Ignis in all her fiery glory.

Her lips pulled back in a heated smile. "My Queen." She tilted her head down and crossed her arm over her chest along with her finger before touching her forehead and meeting my eyes.

"Where did he go? I know he was here!" I shouted at her.

She floated in front of me. She was completely at ease in her element.

"He left, of course."

My jaw snapped shut on the retort. I gritted my teeth for a moment to cool off. An impossibility under the circumstances. "I know that! How?"

"The way all kings travel." She didn't shrug, but it was implied.

I hate this shit.

"He portal," a Fomorian stated, as if that helped.

"He can portal?" I breathed.

"All ruling Kings can. My Queen, Puca was given his freedom. He never ceased to be King." She sat on the edge of the lava lake and ran her fingers through the molten ore as if it was a bath.

"But I could portal, even before I was Queen."

"You are from the Royal line." She rolled her eyes. Sparks flew from her lips as her jaw spit the words out along with embers.

I shook my head. I didn't care about Royal lines or family trees. I watched her without seeing what she was really doing.

"He opened a portal here. Why?" It was the logical question. Sweat ran down my back. My leather legging clung to me, and it itched.

Cinders floated around her, some alight, others black specks. "Fae use fire to teach. You learn or die."

I pushed the bead of sweat on my brow away. "You helped him?" I shouted, "Why? You swore to support my reign," I scoffed as my forehead creased in confusion.

"The cycle of Wyld will never be over as long as Jacques lives. He is a danger to your reign and all Fae. He wanted to find Pil. I helped send him to the surface."

My rage grew as hot as the cavern we now occupied. I sang *Hotel California*. I wanted her to never be able to leave this cave. Everyone who ever came looking for Ignis would be trapped with her.

I touched the underside of her chin as I sang, '*such a lovely face.*' only to stab her in the heart with the dagger Janice left behind.

Her eyes widened in surprise. "My lady," She choked on the liquid rock, leaking from her mouth. Her baking hand grabbed my bicep.

I screamed as the scent of cooking flesh and burned hair filled my nostrils. I raised the blade and dug it into her back again and again. Then, I slashed the hand locked around my arm.

A Fomorian moved in and cleaved the hand from her body. She slipped from the edge of the lake to float on the surface of the molten ore.

"Fire is yours," she coughed, then sank, swallowed by the very fire meant to serve her.

I stood there dumbfounded.

What happens when an elemental is killed?

The lava in the cave churned, growing as intemperate as an ocean storm. It leaped and became a fiery wave. It moved at the speed of lightning.

"We go!" The Fomorians muttered.

My wings wanted to beat down and carry me up to the ceiling. The hot wave grew and it towered over me. I sang for a protection bubble.

My burned arm ached. The ache spread as the hot wave reached the ceiling. The fire engulfed me, and the searing heat became my world. I screamed, as the fire poured in.

Fire burns away all illusions, leaving only the hard truths you never want to see.

My entire body burned with all those truths. There was only one way out of this cave, and that was through the fire.

CHAPTER 24

MERCIA

My parched lip smacked, and my eyes opened. I blinked to clear the scratchy feeling away.

The room came into focus. I was staring at the sleeping face of Nick. He had a collar of some kind on his neck. He was covered in a glamor, one that made him look less Fae, and more changeling.

I smiled.

He's alive!

Tears I didn't want found their way down the sides of my face. I turned my head to see the rest of the room. We were alone, which made me release a heavy breath.

"Nick," I croaked out while trying to move my strapped body. The hard metal of the table pressed into my back.

I smacked my lips together, searching for moisture. My throat worked to swallow, hoping it would ease the pain in my vocal cords.

I closed my eyes to assess my injuries. My throat hurt, but my neck felt fine. My hip felt like pixies chewed on it for a week, but other than that, I was just tired.

I turned back to look at Nick.

I swallowed to clear my throat. Our best hope of getting free was him. I was not strong enough. I probably couldn't even open a can of food.

I hummed for the magic to reveal itself to me.

What I saw jarred me - Nick was on an iron-laced table. The collar around his neck was, too, woven iron, making the skin around the edges to blacken.

His hands and feet were held with iron cuffs. The contact had burned his skin to a char, and his blood was oozing out. It looked red. I knew better than that, but I wondered if they did too.

I tilted to see what was holding me down. It, too, was iron laced. Unlike Nick, it wasn't burning me.

The healing song lingered on the tip of my tongue when the doors slammed open.

I turned my head away from Nick and retched what little contents my stomach held.

"Show me the new witch," the man demanded. He came into view, and all my blood drained from my face.

His glamor was good. Yet, I could see through it as the spell cut through his glamor. He wasn't a warlock. He was a fae.

He glanced over at Nick, his eyes lingering for a moment. A little smirk danced across his lips before he looked around at the doctor.

"So, where is the proof that your little experiment worked?" he demanded.

"She only woke up a few minutes ago. We need a catalyst to trigger her magic," Dr. Chock remarked.

The Fae turned around, "Look, we have been at this for the last two years. You just joined the game."

Oh, Danu, we are fucked!

He was from the Hallowed Hills. He was not a changeling. Only a real Fae would refer to the war as a game.

I glanced over at Nick. His eyes flickered open. He quickly took in the room and then settled on me.

Did he just mouth Mercia?

I pressed my lips closed and moved my head slightly to wave him off.

His eyes darted to the Fae in the room, then they narrowed with his lips pierced.

The Fae sauntered over to Nick and grabbed his chin to turn his head. He inspected Nick's ears. "Where did you get this changeling?" he chuckled.

Nick hissed at the Fae, who smiled back at him.

"Out near one of our farms," Dr. Chock offered.

Funny how she left out the stone bowl.

"And the human?" He asked.

"She was in the city. We never asked why."

Chock is leaving oh so much out.

This was a showing. They wanted a seat at the table. They thought they could join the game, though they were keeping their cards close to their chest.

They didn't know what the bowl was, and they weren't going to tell anyone they had it until they had to.

I closed my eyes.

"How did you manage to capture such a strong changeling? He must have put up quite a fight," the Fae inquired.

"We lost a few. It's irreverent. We can create witches. I can keep this Fae alive for a long time. He will serve two purposes - his bone marrow for new witches and his seed for the next generation."

"I will never fuck one of your skanky witches," Nick growled.

The Fae chuckled. "Give him the blue pills if he doesn't comply. No changeling can stop those. He'll give you all the seed you want."

"Fuck you, you Fae traitor! You work with witches against your own kind?" Nick was shouting now. I knew him enough to know that he would never talk like this.

But if he hadn't said it, I would have.

The words were bursting inside me, along with the idea, they would force him to do anything to propagate witches.

"I hope Oberon and Wyld take you! May Danu curse you where you stand, you two-faced, piece of shit! When Sarah figures out what you're up to, she's going to kill you, slowly. And I'm so going to enjoy watching her do it."

"Those are big words for a surface changeling. And by the way, the rule of Wyld is over, Nicolas," he laughed in Nick's face.

As a response, Nick spat in his eye.

I couldn't hold back, so I laughed.

The Fae stepped back, realizing his mistake. Nick called him a Fae, not a warlock. More importantly, Nick knew who he was.

The Fae recovered and whipped around. "You find the disrespect of a warlock funny," he demanded of me.

I didn't reply. There was no point. I was trapped.

Don't push them any further than necessary!

Plus, it was not like I could fight with the wound in my hip, which was aching more every minute.

"What was it that she said before you put her under?" He asked the doctor.

"I am the predator. All else is prey," Chock remarked, crossing her arms, forcing the white jacket open at the top to reveal a necklace.

I stared up at the ceiling, trying to ease my breathing.

I shouldn't have quoted Momma.

The Fae stared down at my face.

"Finian?" the doctor called to get his attention.

"Put her in an iron room and keep an eye on her! Don't let her out until I speak to you again!" Finian ordered.

Nick laughed, "Something scares you, Finian? Or is it someone? Sarah will kill you! Hunters are the most dangerous of Fae. To them, we are all prey," Nick's laugh followed Finian out the door.

"Put him in his room and give him a blue pill, then send in Bec. She'll get the job done." The doctor released a dry laugh under her breath. A moment later, her eyes landed on me in an appraising fashion. "Do you want to tell me why Finian, the strongest warlock I've ever met, is afraid of you?" She asked.

"Can I have something for the pain?" I demanded.

This was Momma's game - answer questions with questions. I'd just intimated as I was in too much pain to talk.

Now we shall see how she takes this information.

"I could, but you have to give me something first." She leaned in and ran a finger over my left eyebrow.

I grit my teeth. The pain was getting worse. There was no need to fake that. "I don't understand why it matters."

"You scared him. I want to know why."

She was going to hurt me in a minute, and I was going to let her because I wanted her to believe.

Her other hand, the one I couldn't see, dug into the stitches in my hip, holding the flesh together. I howled in agony.

It won't help my throat.

But the magic wasn't working anyway, so it didn't matter.

She worked her thumb deep into the wound. "I've found pain."

I shrieked with blind misery.

"I can trigger the treatments and make you a stronger witch." She pulled her thumb out, giving me a second or two of relief.

I panted with short breaths, opening and closing my eyes. I focused on the healing song. When Nick sang to me. It was the most beautiful sound in all the realms.

"Do you think that the bone marrow transplant works?" She asked, shifting her hand and working two fingers into the wound.

My body was wailing, and my mind stuttered. I closed my eyes and reopened them. I let the memory of Nick's healing me restart, autoplaying in my mind.

I saw him petting my hair back and kissing my forehead. He said, *I hope this works*.

I let her dig into my flesh while I mentally drank the memory.

She pulled her fingers out, and the reprieve began. "Are you ready to tell me something, or should I keep going?"

The doctor definitely liked to torture people. Her irises were dilated, and her breathing was heavy. The scent in the air carried the pheromones of lust.

She gets off on this shit. Yuck!

I loved the hunt. But this was some real psycho Kelpie shit. I whimpered a little. It wasn't fake, though I could hold it back. I didn't. It felt good to let it out, so I embraced the release.

"There was a girl in the CB I was in," I stopped to pant for show. "She used to say that all the time." I bawled, coughing over the CB number.

Just to hide it a little.

The Govs already knew I existed. This way, they could think I overheard someone say it. I figured it might save me.

"What CB?" her hand gripped my hip, squishing the wound together. The pressure felt good at first. However, the steady pressure grew until it became painful.

The scent of persimmons and cilantro curled around us.

It's hers.

I could smell her magic. I blinked to push that information away. I needed to keep my head in the game. I didn't want to say Cassidy's CB. I couldn't have anyone brought to identify me. I looked human there.

Just as I do now.

She stopped pressing and wrenched the wound open like a hand-hold on a rock face. Shrieking filled the room. I couldn't stop myself. The feeling of having one's flesh forcibly ripped open is pure torment.

I began repeating *twinkle, twinkle little stars* out loud without the proper rhythm to throw her off. It also gave me a focal point for the pain.

"Do you think that spell can hurt me?" She cackled like the little witch she was. "Your throat is too sore to sing a proper spell. So, tell me, what CB?" her soft tone was turning from coax to the harsh edge of anger.

Like most psychos, she liked to get her way and didn't want it to take too long. Unless, of course, that it was her choice. She dug her fingers back into my wound to regain control.

I obliged her by hollering in pain. The high that she had moments before returned, and she dug a little deeper, making me scream a little more.

Momma said all torture has a rhythm, that you have to find it and keep it going. She said that killing someone is an art form. And most importantly, she taught me that letting your prey feel like they are in charge is the first real step to winning.

Whoever Finian was, he understood exactly what Momma's mantra meant. He'd be back to either kill me or make me swear an oath.

And he won't come alone.

This was the moment. "CB 196. Larka." I appeared to blurt, "It was her CB. She was our witch." I was panting again.

Dr. Chock pulled her fingers out of the wound in my leg and patted the side of my face with her bloody hand.

"That's a good girl. I knew you'd give it up to me." She ran her hands over my body, and giggled then turned her back on me.

Part of me wanted to kill her right there. However, I had to wait. I could feel my hunter side growing stronger. Instead of attacking, I squeezed my eyes shut to push the tears away and waited.

Dr. Chock fiddled with something just out of sight and returned with some blood orange-looking liquid with which she wiped off the gash on my hip.

"Don't look so worried. It's iodine to disinfect your wound. I'll stitch you up and let you rest in a nice iron-lined room." Her hand had a rounded needle in it.

She stung me with it as it dug in. I hissed to keep from crying.

The hormones flooding my system had ramped up my entire body, making me shaky. I whimpered a bit to make it look good. She kept getting her rocks off on my pain, therefore, I remained docile.

For the first time in days, I felt stronger, even with the injury.

I lay back, and waited for her to finish. My breathing slowed as the adrenaline burned away.

Is this what they did to Larka?

Chock was a patter. She patted you as if that would make up for her psycho bedside manner. This time, instead of patting my face, she patted my breast.

Her inappropriate touching made me wonder if she's into more than just torture to get her rocks off.

"All done!" She leaned down and planted a wet kiss on my lips. "Don't worry, if you survive, you will learn to like me," she said smiling.

I blinked as if I was a cat that didn't understand the crazy human's weird ramblings.

"There's just one more thing before I put you to bed for the night." She pulled the rubber gloves off with a snap. She moved out of my sight to the far side of the room.

My hearing had improving, so the sound of tumblers tripping over the locking system of a safe playing its simple song in the background.

It was sad, really. Such a powerful witch and she couldn't even whistle a lock open.

Neither could I right now, but that was only because I was no longer strong enough.

At least I know how.

I could hear the song of the bowl before I saw it. The song was strong, and with all the pain I just endured, it would only get stronger.

My breathing never hitched, and I kept my eyes on the ceiling, waiting for her to announce what she planned to do with that bowl. I was biting my lip, since I couldn't react.

If I do, I'll never leave this room.

The doctor set the bowl down on the table next to me with a clink. I used that sound as an excuse to glance over. She loosened the strap holding my arms down, but not the cuffs keeping me in check. My fingers didn't touch. I couldn't reach anything. She loosened me just enough to do nothing.

"Here, hold this and tell me what you think." She put the heavy bowl in my hands and crossed her arms.

Her belief that I was weak disturbed me. I was used to being underestimated, but not to this degree.

It's a bit insulting.

My hand cupped the cool stone, and an electric jolt shot up my arms, working its way through my body. Its song called to me, whispering a desire. It wanted me to do something, yet I didn't know what. The *what* was just out of reach.

The colors of stone fascinated me, and I lifted the bowl a little bit to get a good look at it - crystal, agate, jasper, granite, and other rocks I couldn't name were layered one over the other.

So this is the big secret I'm charged with keeping.

I was the keeper. Momma only told me we were to keep it safe from all save Puca, until he asked for it. But until that moment, I'd never even seen the damn thing. Magic curled in my belly.

It wants me to do something.

I let the only thing I could say trip out of the hole in my face, "It's pretty."

Chock slapped me, then patted the same spot as if to make it all better. Blood rushed to that side of my face, heating it under her hand.

With a wicked smile, she said, "I don't care what it looks like. Do you feel something or hear anything?" She uncrossed her arms and pushed her white hair out of her face.

Her hair wasn't gray. Funny, I'd thought it was. No, her hair was white.

I turned the bowl to see how the overhead light played through the lighter rock that rainbowed the bottom of the bowl.

"Am I supposed to hear something?" I asked, then cringed away for good measure.

She yanked the bowl from my grasp, and I held back from reaching for it.

A fresh pain started in my belly.

Pixies must have moved in only to chew their way out.

A fine sheen of sweat glossed my skin.

She clunked the bowl on the table next to us and placed the back of her hand to my forehead.

"Don't die. That would really suck."

I didn't turn away this time. Instead, I expelled golden bile onto the table and convulsed as my body tried to push out more. Before I knew it, she was pushing my table down a rocky earthen hallway, further away from the object of my salvation.

The magic wakes around me didn't go away. Normally, after such a traumatic episode, the song would dissipate.

The grinding in my belly kept the pain-meter set to medium-low, and my ability to use magic would only grow exponentially.

She moved me through several doors, all guarded by humans with a drop of Fae blood. Finally, we came to a stop at the end of a hall with only one door. Dr. Chock smiled her simpering fake smile at the human standing there.

"How's it going in there? Is he done?"

The guard shook his head, glanced at her then looked at the floor.

"What is the hold-up?" she huffed. "The blue pill worked, right? So he should be done."

The guard pulled the slot in the door open and tilted his head for her to take a look.

She scrunched her nose, "You know I don't like men." She shoved him to the side, peeked inside, and sighed.

"Get it cleaned up! Meanwhile, we'll put her in there. I don't think he'll kill her. She's innocent," she said with scorn.

I gulped.

Nick killed some chick? Holy shit!

That was not Nick's style at all. He usually left the girl-killing to me.

Dr. Chock loosened my restraints, and as the guard pulled me off the table, he gripped my neck so tight I could barely breathe.

Dr. Chock opened the door, and the guard shoved me in. I tumbled to the floor, landing on my hip, and yelped in pain.

"You fuckers!" I screamed. The sound bounced off the walls and was returned by a deep growl.

On the other side of the room was a black and brown speckled wolf. And judging by the number of teeth he's sporting, he was not happy. *At all!*

CHAPTER 25

SARAH

When you're sick and have a fever, your eyes are hot, scratchy, and your body feels like you've sat in a hot tub for too long, or fell asleep in a sauna. Your mouth is dry, and no matter how much water you drink, the thirst cannot be quenched.

This was worse.

I was a frog in a pot, and the pot was filled with lava. It was cooking me, only I wasn't cooking.

The burning pain from before wasn't there. I expected my nerve endings to shriek with agony. But yeah, nothing.

I was in the pot with the boiling lava water, and it wasn't going to kill me.

The vision of Ignis slipping beneath the surface of the lava played over in my mind.

I give you fire.

She'd said those words before when I was fighting Nikki. Afterwards, I was able to throw fireballs. But I never explored the use of fire further.

Because what was the point? I was Queen and had all the elements at my disposal.

The rule of Wyld wasn't over, or so she said. I didn't want to believe that. Even if Jacques was alive, Wyld was done. I killed it.

Didn't I?

Ignis didn't think so, and she was willing to die to stop it. I was willing to kill to stop Jacques. What was the real difference?

The heat radiating in my body was nothing more than a barely contained furnace of power. My body pounded in time with my heart, and my heart made the heat. It was one big circle of life.

I sat up, and my hair pulled free of my lava bath. The black strands glowed with an internal force before settling back into the dark tresses Fae had given me.

The lava lake had a thin skin. In some places the lava had cooled only to reform into a malleable rock or Playdough. I was like that Playdough, hot and on the verge of melting back into the puddle.

Somehow, I managed to stand without sinking into the ichorous liquid underneath. Before I could think about another thing, I flashed to the nearest ledge and took in the cavern.

The surrounding magic had not changed. It still waked in its eternal vibrations, reaching out to each other, blending and merging. There was one big difference though. It was the single opening in the cavern ceiling. It was a deep hole, one that held a light far above.

I didn't stop to think what that light meant. I did what I always do - I moved forward toward the fight.

My wings beat with my desires and carried me as far as I dared. The top was still far away, but there was no doubt in my mind where it led. The scent of motor oil and trash grew stronger with every beat of my wings. That was the surface. The light was somehow different. I clung to the walls to wait.

When the sun goes down, I will see.

The sunset on the surface came, and I emerged from the hole. There, laying on the ground, not far away, was a single changeling - Young and weak in magic. He blinked with fright.

"I didn't come here to kill you. Where is Jacques?" I asked.

The boy pointed to his mouth which he opened wide. He couldn't answer. There wasn't enough tongue left to reply.

The cut looked jagged. He drew a picture of a knife and his mouth.

They'd cut it out.

Tears threatened at the corners of my eyes. I cupped his chin with my hand, "Which way did he go?" I asked as my throat thickened.

The child pointed up.

I hummed for the hunter's trail to guide my way. Jacques' silvery trail lit up the sky and ended. I surveyed the area, hoping for a lead, then turned back to the child.

"Was Janice with him, a violet-eyed warrior?"

The boy nodded vigorously. He pointed up and used his hand to display an explosion.

Rounds float, portals explode.

They were on a round. He used it to travel somewhere through a portal.

I stepped closer to the child and grabbed his chin, forcing his mouth open. I stared into the child's eyes and found what I needed to heal him.

Compassion.

That was what Fae lacked and why they could only heal those they loved.

They lack compassion.

I found it for this boy and sang the song of healing.

As his little pink tongue regrew, tears tracked their way down my face.

The child cried and wiggled to get away. But I didn't stop until finally, the tip formed and took hold. I released him, and he fell to the ground.

"Please," he sputtered, then froze to stare up at me.

I crouched down next to him, and he dove into my arms.

"Thank you!" He muttered over the tears and snot escaping from his face.

I forced him to look at me. I didn't need his thanks. He was too human to see that as a changeling, he shouldn't ask for it.

"How long ago did they leave?"

"Two," he coughed. "Two years ago. I've been waiting here."

I stepped back and almost lost my footing. There was a hut not far away with a light in the window and plants growing in rows. The child was about ten years old. He was thin, his eyes hollowed from starvation and malnutrition. I didn't wait for him to say another word. I sang for the farmer in the dell to bring a cow, a pig and vegetables, turning the hut into a house and the garden into an oasis of food.

The boy refused to let me go and kept murmuring *thank you*. I gulped back the desire to say, *your welcome*.

I pulled him away from my body and held his arms, "You should never thank anyone for doing the right thing."

He bit his lip and nodded his head as tears spilled down his face. "You're the Queen, aren't you?"

"Yes."

"He—Jacques said he was going to kill you, that the purple-eyed warrior was his bait."

I knew this already.

There was nothing more to learn here. Jacques was gone, and so was his trail. You couldn't track a portal.

I petted the kid's hair back from his face. "I'll send someone to take care of you," I remarked. It would be a perfect job for mom.

"Can you wait for them?" I asked.

He rubbed the tears away and nodded in agreement.

I pushed him toward the house I'd created and the flourishing garden. Then jumped over the edge of the hole back down to my fiery cave. I closed the hole behind me as I went.

There will be no more escaping this way.

The best way to find anyone on the surface was Nick.

Only he, too, is in trouble.

I headed back to my castle and the library. Mom was there, and so was any hope for answers.

CHAPTER 26

MERCIA

I scampered back from the huge animal, pacing on the other side of the cell. There was a dead body on the floor next to me. A woman.

She was slightly touched by Fae. Not much, but only enough to cause trouble. Her brilliant diamond-colored eyes resembled the uncut stone more than the sparkling jewel.

Her blood never sprouted even one mushroom. It pooled red all around what was left of her neck. The exposed portion of her spinal cord was utterly destroyed, leaving a small portion of skin and tendon holding her head to her body.

I looked from the collared wolf to the body and back. Its teeth dripped with blood-soaked saliva. He snapped his jaw, and roped drool broke off, landing on my bare leg. Then, he growled a little more before sitting down.

The wolf whined and lowered his head, hiding his green eyes in shame. He nuzzled the side of a leg. The blue blood from his wound slowed. There were mushrooms sprouting from the droplets. The chains holding him to the walls had slipped from his limbs.

Puca was the only Fae I'd heard of that could change shapes. Nick was his father's son. He could deny it all he wanted, but for once, I was grateful it was true.

He was free of the chains, but he couldn't sing with the collar on. The fur around the collar was gone, and the skin edged in black, matted and burned. The sickly scent of burned hair lingered in the air.

I gulped, then tried to remove it. The iron burned the tips of my fingers. Nick moved away from me, yipping.

The collar was laced with iron and it was too much for hair or fur. But not enough to break the skin on its own. Judging from the blue blood oozing around the edges, it was causing a great deal of pain.

He limped toward me and sniffed the wound in my thigh. The stitches were red and inflamed. He licked my hand.

I ran my hands over his head and cupped his joules, forcing him to look at me.

"I can't take the collar off, and you can't heal me this time. We are in the deepest pixie shit of all time. Fae-fucked. For. Sure." I whispered.

Nick nudged my cheek as I tried to stop the tears from falling. He pushed me toward the door.

This was not part of my plan. My plan was to use Nick to open a portal and escape together with the bowl.

"No, I can't leave you," I mourned.

This more human than human shit sucked. I pushed the black and white hair out of my face. Nick licked the dry blood from my cheek. He then pushed again and nipped. He limped around behind me, rubbing his nose up and down my back as he urged me to go.

"Can't you change back? Your dad does it all the time." I asked in frustration.

Nick shook his shaggy head. It hit me. He didn't know how.

It's hard to reproduce magic if you don't understand how it happened to begin with.

I used the uneven portions of the wall as handholds to stand. Keeping my weight on my one good leg, I hobbled toward the door.

Iron bracketed the frame and held the slabs of wood together. It wasn't enough to stop magic. Nevertheless, a smirk curled one side of my face.

Stupid witches.

Agony shot through my hip. I'd shifted my weight over and shouldn't have. I leaned back toward the wall and whistled at the door. The lock lifted, and a loud click filled our little space before the latch lowered.

It didn't work.

Pixies shit!

I glanced at Nick. He nudged my hand to encourage me. I straightened my back and shook my arms, then cleared my throat. Wetting my lips, I put them together, and blew. The whistle was clear.

Though I couldn't see the magic, I could picture the wakes hitting the lock and releasing the mechanism. A click followed, and the door sagged open a fraction of an inch. With one finger touching only the wood, I eased it open.

Before I could get far, Nick slipped past me and down the hall. He leaped onto the first body he came to. I couldn't tell if the guy was human or warlock.

I. Didn't. Care.

They were all a threat to humanity and Fae. Anyone helping these animals was a threat, and I wouldn't leave one alive.

I hummed the gun out of the other human's hand with *Come back, Peter, Come back, Paul,* before he could get a shot off.

The weapon landed in my waiting palm, and I quickly dispensed with the second human by easing a hole through his chest cavity and out the other side. The bullet hit the rocky wall behind with a crack. The man's body fell back against the surface and slid down, leaving a smear of red human blood in his wake.

Nick cuffed at me in appreciation.

"The bowl is in the operation room in a safe."

Even injured, Nick was lighter on his feet as a canine than Fae, and he moved too fast for my limping form. My wounded hip did nothing more than leave a leg to drag behind me.

I sang for *light as a feather* to help myself. But my magic was less than before Puca gave me my choice. And the song barely gave me the lift I needed. I sang it again for an extra layer, and my pep increased a bit more.

"I guess I should be grateful for what I can get," I remarked under my breath.

Nick cuffed at me in agreement. His fur was a sleek black with touches of brown that laced his belly.

The hair on his head was soft. Most dogs I'd petted had coarse fur, and it only grew more so as you reached the underbelly. Nicks didn't have the normal course dry look to it. It looked as soft as sable.

I pulled my thoughts from his coat to the end of the hallway and what lay on the other side of that door.

The handle turned as we reached it, and the voice grew from the other side.

I smelled her before I saw her. She had that cloying scent of persimmons mixed with the soap of cilantro. Dr. Chock's voice carried, "We need answers about the bowl, and only that Fae can give it to us," she remarked.

The door swung open, and her eyes widened at the sight of us. Nick leaped past me, knocking the witch to the floor. His teeth sank into her neck with a crunch, cutting off any further chance for her to speak or sing.

She didn't need to sing. The bowl was calling. Its sweet ring beat against the walls. The pain gnawing in my belly ramped up, and I splayed my hand over the growing hole inside me.

The magic was eating away at my inside. I doubled over panting. I shook my head to get back in the fight, pushing myself upright.

Nick shook his head violently as he tore out Chock's throat. Bright blue blood splattered everywhere, coating the walls and anyone within a two-foot radius.

The second person was a man, a warlock. I sang for *the London bridge to fall down*. The magic took hold and knocked him to the floor, just as fast as a rock thrown from a tall building.

The two humans guarding the door raised the alarm. Nick made short work of one.

There, lying on the floor, between the two dead bodies, was the stone bowl of Danu.

The second guard punched me in the head, and I collided into the door frame with a crack.

For a moment, stars shone in my eyes, and the sound of Nick attacking the human was all I could make out. The dizziness slipped away with the first slap I made to one side of my face. My eyes cleared.

With the second, I sang for Jack to make me nimble and quick. The elusive magic took hold and the power of a Jack song infused my body. However, I pulled a *twinkling star* for good measure. It wrapped me in the darkest sky lit by the brightest stars, giving me a fresh hit of energy. Then, I sang a song of *sixpence*. It hit like the adrenaline from before, only this time it was for the thrill of the kill, not fear of the hunt.

Nick jumped for the guard, who threw his arm up to keep the wolf at bay. Two more humans joined the fight, attempting to make it through the bottleneck of the doorway.

My magic wasn't enough to protect us. The gun had slipped from my grasp when I hit my head. So I sang for *the old man and his rain.* Water bubbled up from the floor and began filling the room. A moment later, the crack of a gun sliced the air.

The feeling of being stabbed hit my arm, lighting my nerve ending on fire.

I looked down to see red/blue blood flowing not only from my shoulder but my thigh, where they'd drilled into my hip and thigh bones.

I sang for the wounds to close. The man standing in front of me was still trying to hold Nick at bay.

"Let him come!" I ordered.

This was one spell that wouldn't fall flat. It was in my blood and part of what I was. No amount of magic could take a hunter's ability to fight.

Nick released the man and darted around the guy, bumping him as he went for the other two.

The guard fell forward. I grabbed his arm where he was bleeding and hummed for the hunter's curse.

I found a straw once from before the fall. It was made of metal. Humans used it to suck up a drink. Riding his blood was me sucking up his life like a drink.

The hole in my shoulder ceased to bleed and closed. The wound on my hip stopped bleeding as well, and the ache eased somewhat.

The magic transferred his life to me. His eyes darkened and hallowed. His skin sank in on itself and turned paper-thin.

When I released the man, he was shrunken and old, his teeth falling out of his head. He blinked at me and moaned, "Fae."

I pulled my hand away from his arm. I was covered in new markings, unlike the ones from before. They were more intricate.

The world had returned to the waking one I'd known. I pulled the weapons belt from the guy's shrunken waist and strapped it on over my hospital gown.

"Nick," I called.

His teeth sank into the chest of our last opponent, his jaw closed, and he pulled back, shaking his head, and tearing the flesh away from the skeleton. The red blood of a human sprayed anew over the top of the blue.

The walls were like a Jackson Pollock painting, minus the yellows.

Nick lifted his head. His jaw was covered with gore, and he wagged his tail, creating a thumping sound against the heavy wooden door.

The water came up to mid-calf. I took a step forward. I needed to touch Nick. I wanted him to wrap me in his arms, or I him. Either way would work for me.

I could close his wounds at the very least.

Nick moved to meet me in the middle when my big toe came in contact with what could only be the cold stone of the bowl.

My momentum froze. My foot sank back down. In a blink of an eye, all that forward motion bled away like the lives lost on the floor.

I was lost to the song of the bowl and my oath to magic.

My master controls my every move.

My body bent over. There was nothing I could do to stop what I was doing. Both hands cupped the bowl as I brought it out of the water. The murky blood-laced liquid slopped over the side and ran down my arms to drip off my elbows.

"Shoot her! Now!" Finian yelled from the doorway.

My eyes met Nick's black orbs. His fur was melting back into his naked skin as his body morphed back into his Fae form. The iron collar held fast to his neck and blood still wept from his hip.

He couldn't use magic to fight. He turned to deal with them.

I shifted the bowl to my left hand and tossed the dagger I'd taken off the dead guy at him.

"Nick!" I shouted.

He snatched it from the air between a finger and his thumb. He quickly went to work on the witches.

My throwing hand was still extended, closed in a partial fist. As I opened it, my fingers splayed wide, and a humming vibration grew in my belly. It climbed its way into my throat and flew over my tongue, tickling the hairs in my nose. The wakes hit the wall with a force I'd never experienced, and I ripped a portal into the earthen wall.

"GO!" Nick's deep tenor urged me.

I couldn't control my actions. I turned to look at Nick attacking the witches. Someone shot him with a tranquilizer gun and Nick slumped to the floor. A scream ripped from my throat as the magic pulled me through.

I landed on a sitting room floor next to a couch covered in flora print fabric.

The scream still tore at my throat. I leaped to my feet with the stone bowl cradled under my off arm and a throwing dagger in my other hand.

The tinkle of porcelain touching broke the quiet, and I circled to face the rest of the room. Puca sat shirtless in a side chair with his legs crossed, holding a cup of tea. His chest carried five slices diagonally across the exposed skin. All I could hear was the leather of his pants squeaking.

"Don't dirty the carpet. Set the bowl on the coffee table and go clean up," he instructed, then waved me off.

I jumped to the other side of the coffee table, ready to shout him down and demand he return me.

"How did I get here?" I thrust my hand out like before, but nothing happened. I wiggled my fingers and flexed my hand open and closed.

Puca didn't reply. He merely slicked his hair back. "An interesting question for later."

The magic had other ideas. It drug me through the cottage in a flash and out into the backyard, where a bath awaited me.

Before I could say how do you do, I was unceremoniously shoved into the water, and my clothes snapped away. When I finally came up, a blond changeling stood over me. Her blue eyes sparkled with joy.

I snarled at her. "Where am I? Who are you?"

She shoved me back under the water, pulled me back up, and began scrubbing my hair.

"You are just like your mother. Pil was all business too." She kissed the top of my head. "I'm Maryann. This is my father's cottage - the safest place in the Hallowed Hills."

As if I should know this.

Before I could answer, she again shoved me under the water to rinse my hair. When I finally came back up, I sang a protection shield around myself.

Her hands bounced off. "No need to be rude. I was only helping, so the magic didn't drown you. Father gets his way no matter what." She chided and waggled a finger at me as if I was a naughty child in need of scolding.

"I have to go back. Nick needs me!" I shouted and attempted to stand.

Her eyes fell to her lap, and the reality of who she really was hit me. The blond hair and saucer blue eyes, her reference to her father. She was *the Alice,* the one from the songs. She was Puca's daughter. But she looked too human, and she said her name was Maryann.

How can she be so human?

The magic pushed me back into the water.

"You can't leave until you're clean, Mercia. Just let me help you finish, and then Puca will see you," she meekly informed me.

The water running down my face hid my tears.

They wouldn't let me save him. The Queen said the Fae realm was closed for all time to the surface. Nick said I wouldn't be allowed to leave. There was no way out of the

Hallowed Hills. He and Puca were the only ones able to travel between.

Momma never spoke of how she got out. I never thought to ask her. There was a myriad of things I didn't ask about. I would just have to add this one to an ever-growing list.

The color of the water blurred before me from just a dingy brown to a reddish-blue as all the blood and dirt mixed.

How am I ever going to save anyone trapped down here?

My list of failures never got shorter -Ron, now Nick.

Who cares about a stupid bowl or a dumb wand?

Real people were dying, and the only reason I couldn't save them was because the Queen said so.

My gaze shifted around, looking for answers that weren't there. They were never going to be in a garden in Fae. This place was a land of fantasy. Everyone living here was living a dream.

It's like they're all asleep.

My vision caught on the color of my marking. No longer was I covered in just the hunter's green. Now, it was intertwined with a light green, one I'd always associated with Nick.

I carry the blood of both lines in me now.

I might have had my magic back, but Puca was in control, and like the petulant child I was being treated, I wanted to stomp my feet and scream.

And scream, I will, because everyone needs to wake up from this dreamland.

CHAPTER 27

SARAH

"My Queen, there is nothing here of use," Lavender stated with irritation. She threw a journal across the room which hit a shelf and landed on the floor with a plop.

"There has to be something!" I shouted and my anger pushed Lavender into the stone floor.

Mom put her hand on my shoulder, "Control, Sarinha," she whispered.

She wanted me to calm down. I couldn't. I didn't want to hurt anyone, but I couldn't stop Jacques if I didn't know what he was up to. My irritation bubbled up inside me and spilled over onto anyone in the room.

My wings flared, and it was all I could do to stop them from pushing everything in the room down. I'd grown stronger over time. Controlling my emotions was harder than it would appear. There was a constant burning in my blood, fueling my rage.

As Queen, I felt everything more. It was as if I was tuned into the magic at its very core.

I rolled my head around on my shoulders and listened to the tunes of the room - the books and the shelves, the crystal in the windows, and the branches and roots lining the walls. They all sang to me. It brought a calmness, one I needed. Without Janice, I was dancing on a slack rope, hoping I didn't misstep.

I blink back at those desires. Was this the reason why Puca dances everywhere? To keep his emotions in order?

I shook my head.

Who knows the why's of Puca's behavior?

I couldn't even figure out what his plan ultimately was.

"Danu created the stone with magic," Alice stated, and Lavender nodded her head in agreement.

I pinched the bridge of my nose rather than explain how wrong they were.

"Yes," Lavender said to mom, urging her on.

"She also made the stone bowl and a wand," my mother paced from the desk to where the journals were stacked to the nearest shelf, then, just like her father, pivoted and returned. "She called the bowl a focal point and the wand the anchor," she continued but stopped her pacing and glanced at the doorway and the walls.

"I have held both the wand and the bowl." Mom looked at me, then quickly to the floor.

"When? Where?" I demanded.

"We are the witches of Oberon," She chanced a glance up at me. Her blue eyes didn't hide the fear she housed inside. "Every witch in our line was sworn to keep the bowl and wand safe until Oberon called for them." She went and sat in a chair to face away from me.

"Should I leave?" Lavender whispered.

"No." I waved her to a chair behind me. "You've never told me anything about the past, your family, my father. I don't even know where you were born!" I shouted. The wakes around my mother smooth as if to disappear.

That is mom's specialty - hiding.

She did it for years.

And she did it for me.

"We don't have time for a game of family feud. So if you could get to the important parts, that would be great," I stated.

"My mother, Demelza, told me that we were the Keepers of the Bucket and the Handle. Those were the simple terms for the stone bowl and the wand." She took a deep breath, then continued "I don't know what they do. Neither did my mother. Our bloodline was to keep them safe, that is all.

Only Puca knows. Maw never even told me who my father was. I only found out after she died."

My wings flared and closed several times, waiting for mom, Alice, Allison, fucking Maryann to give me something I could work with.

With all the names she'd used, I was hoping she would at least give me a starting point of where to find these items.

"I can't tell you where I was born because I don't know. I don't know if I was born here, in Fae, or on the surface. Puca didn't say, and neither did Maw." She turned around to look at me, her eyes brimming with tears.

My mother spent most of my childhood on the verge of tears for one reason or another. I normally brushed it away. That was before…before I touched magic, before I was Queen.

She told a very different story now. She was terrified. The wakes around her shivered in fear.

I kneeled in front of her and took her hands. "Mom, I'm," I stopped. I couldn't say it. Our eyes met, and she nodded in time with me. A small smile pulled the edges of her lips.

"I can't either," she murmured.

I kissed her knuckles and gazed up at her. "But you understand?"

She pressed her lips flat to keep them from trembling and nodded her head.

"Maw buried the bowl near a moon circle in a place called Ireland. I later hid the wand on a statue nearby." She brushed her tears away.

A little piece of my heart envied her for those freely falling tears. I envied her for being so open about her feelings without a worry about how they might be used against her.

"The only person who knows where they are now is Pil or Mercia," she said and sagged in her seat.

The information was not the release I'd hoped for. Pil was not on our side. She would've given them to Jacques had she lived.

"How did Pil get them?"

"Well, she found the wand. I gave her the bowl."

"Mom! What the fuck for?" I yelled.

"My father told me to. I am not capable of protecting them. I am still the mother. There is only you and me. There was supposed to be a crone too," she mourned, pushing her hair back out of her face with one hand.

"What are you talking about?" I pulled my hands from hers and turned away.

This was no different than my entire childhood. Mom talking about crazy shit that made no sense. I ran my hand over my hair down to my neck and groaned as I tilted my head back.

"I'm not doing a very good job of explaining, am I?" she asked and caved in on herself.

This was what she did. She'd say something weird out of context without explaining it.

"You're the three?" Lavender asked.

Mom blinked and smiled, her head bobbing up and down. "Yes. There were supposed to be three of us - Maiden, Mother, and Crone. My mother died before you were born. As long as there were three of us, we could keep the bowl and wand safe, which is curious because even when I was growing up, there were only the two of us. But Maw died, and then there was just me. I was alone." She looked away.

"I could have protected them, whatever they are!" I yelled. "Now Jacques could have them. Fuck, mom! Mercia isn't our ally."

The walls silvered with my anger. I didn't know what the hell the stupid bowl and wand did, but I wouldn't have given them to Pil.

"Stop shouting! The entire castle can hear you," Puca laughed and handed me back the red stoned ring.

I turned on him, angry I hadn't heard him come in. I didn't even feel the magic opening the portal. Usually, the wakes in a space would shift just before they separate.

Without another thought, I slammed Puca against a wall. "You gave Pil the stone bowl and wand?" I growled.

Puca wasted not one moment and wrapped my throat with a daisy chain to cut off my air supply.

I pulled him back to me with the rumble in my belly and forced him to his knees at my feet. "You may not answer to me, but you will tell me why you would endanger everyone by giving Pil the keeping of my birthright."

I pushed his head down, revealing the back of his neck. The skin covering him shivered and changed to fur. No longer did a Fae kneel before me, but a snapping beast.

He darted for one of my wings. I opened a portal that let out on the other side of the room, then trapped him in a bubble. He rammed his head into the protection shield and fell back a Fae.

The rumble of his laughter echoed in the rafters.

"Sarinha, I give up. Good fight, though." He snapped his fingers, and the shield fell around him like soap bubbles. "Pil was my sworn vassal." He pulled his hand up to clean his nails, then blew on them for good measure.

"You? You were the one she swore to for all time?" I scoffed. "Why didn't you give them to me?" I demanded.

"What if you died? They would then belong to the King, to Wyld, to Jacques." He leaned over just enough to make it appear he was going to bow but didn't.

"Leave your mother be. She was never meant to protect the bowl and wand. Demelza broke the bloodline long before Alice was born. Stop bothering her." He extended his hand to my mother.

Mom ran to her father and took the offering, allowing it to engulf her tiny fingers. She gazed up at Puca with such adoration, it made me a little sick.

"But why Pil?"

"Because she was the strongest Fae on the surface, a skilled assassin and killer. Her wit would have kept them safe for far longer than any of us could."

He opened a portal in front of us and pulled out a stone bowl. The room was engulfed in a song, one that waked into my bones.

A thump drew my attention to The Keeper, it was slumped against a nearby wall. It murmured something and quickly darted into the stacks heading as far away from the bowl as possible.

A rainbow of rock made up the stone on the bottom, giving it a translucent effect at times.

"Where did you get that?" I asked in awe.

"Mercia. I told you she would not turn on us. Do you believe me now, granddaughter?" He asked with a cocked eyebrow to go with his cocky attitude.

"What about the wand?" I retorted and reached for the bowl.

He pulled it back. "Until Jacques is dead, my dear Queen, none may touch the stone bowl of Danu, save myself and Mercia, for we are bound to its keeping."

I wanted to protest. But I'd already made a fool of myself.

Puca let me win that fight.

I was taking my frustration out on everyone in the room.

Puca moved to my side and tipped my chin up. "Do you feel better?" he whispered at me, not to me, in my ear. He wasn't trying to compel me.

I stared him down, then looked away. He petted the side of my face. "All Queens need a foil to fight. Janice was yours. I was Danu's. I will stand in if needs be or we can find a different kind of release for your pent-up frustrations." His eyes twinkled with mischievousness, and his brows waggled. "I believe your father has the quarry you were searching for." His chuckle echoed in the room like a dark cavern. It carried from one side to the other.

CHAPTER 28

SARAH

I expected Puca to lead me to Cernunnos and whatever he'd found.

Instead, the horse's ass opened a portal and left without saying another word, taking the stone bowl with him.

The irony was that I didn't even think to ask about the wand. I was too angry he'd left. Usually, when Puca left, I was relieved. Just being around him gave me a headache.

My eyes fell on Mom and my little plan for her. The boy needed protection. Mom was good at that with kids.

I'd forgotten to ask his name. I mentally smacked myself in the head.

"My Queen?" Lavender inquired with a raised eyebrow.

"Yeah," I sighed, resisting the urge to pinch the bridge of my nose.

"There is a messenger here."

My head swung around to greet the poor soul, only there wasn't another person in the room save my mother, Lavender, and the Record Keeper/creeper.

Lavender's gaze flitted to the arched doorway, then back to me. She'd changed her hair color again. This time, it was a soft buttery yellow, the shade found in frosting and faded rose pedals. It suited her far more than her normal fair of bright and distracting.

If Lavender felt good enough for a new hairdo, maybe things were looking up. My eyes widened at the thought. Maybe Janice was still here, in the Hallowed Hills, and that was the message.

The person standing in the archway waited with a lowered head.

The spark of hope died, right where it should have. Nothing would ever be that easy, not for me. Not in Fae, not ever.

I clamped my jaw down on the bitten flavor and faced the messenger.

Don't kill her, no matter what she says.

It was Mod and she couldn't enter.

There was no way I was letting anyone else in here, so I sauntered out into the hallway. Mod pressed against the wall as I passed and followed behind me.

I led her away from the library and into the *stairway to heaven* room. Wenn lay on his back with his pudgy legs crossed and his fingers twiddling over his chest.

Has it been two days?

I couldn't remember. But Wenn's time was up. He'd sat in that bubble long enough, and it was time to go.

As Michael Corleone said, '*all debts are settled today.*'

"Well?"

He jumped to his feet and stared me down. He only had one good eye. The other was scrunched partially shut. A scent cloud of rotten meat and congealed blood hung around him.

"If I take the hat off, I die. If I leave it on, you'll kill me. There ain't no good choices," he huffed.

My hand grew hot with an inner fire, and the glow lit up the room.

This is new.

Wenn pulled the bloody hat from his head and worked his fingers around the edge. He snarled at me and extended the one hand holding the disgusting thing. After that, with a flick of his wrist, he tossed it out of the bubble.

A fireball leapt from my palm, cooking and then burning the wretched thing. The hat disintegrated into ash.

So focused on the hat, I missed Wenn's regression. The child I expected to be standing there turned out to be a teenager. He was small for his age, and he shined with the magic of Fae.

He glared up at me.

"I remember the choice," he replied and offered nothing else.

If I didn't know how many humans he'd killed, I would laugh at how Fae he really was.

But fair is fair, and as Janice had explained - unless you are fair, life won't be.

The red stoned ring encased one of my fingers, aching to be used. This was a purpose I could get behind.

"For all your many crimes against humanity and Fae, I will take the one thing you didn't know you possessed yet threw away - your magic."

I pointed the ring at him and pulled whatever magic lingered in his system out. Danu called it a mineral. For me, all I could see was where the wakes moved from him to the ring.

The stone beat with his heart, and he cried with the loss. Eventually, the shine disappeared, leaving only a human child.

He never stopped crying.

I opened a portal to the surface, to a place Nick told me about, and I shoved him through. After that, I dusted my hands off.

Mod led me out the main doors to the courtyard and a round.

"We are going to the edges of the Hallowed Hills. It is a place where Wyld runs and never ceases," she supplied no more information.

I glanced down at her mushroom round and smirked. There was no way I was riding that thing, not when I could get there under my own power.

"Lead the way."

The day-glow light of Fae illuminated the Hallowed Hills in a way that never ceased to enthrall me. The outline of the leaves glowed in the light, and the flowers soaked it up.

There was no high noon or midnight, only dawn and dusk. The raising and lowering of the enchanted stalagmites were lining the ceiling. Furthermore, the ceiling was covered in curlicues and scrolling circles, a feature that marked Fae in many places.

We arrived at the outskirts of the hills to a crowd. Cernunnos baritone rumbled, echoing off the rocky walls not yet smoothed by magic.

"Where is your master?" he growled.

The crowd twittered behind their hands and smiled plastic barbie doll smiles. Their tilted eyes, hair, and marking, showed the true colors of each and every person.

The white hair of the UnSeelie dotted the landscape. They were not alone. The Seelie with their dark coloring were also present in numbers.

The Fae were bigger gossips than a group of old ladies at the Friday night bingo parlor. Word had spread fast of Cernunnos cornered quarry.

I waited for the Fae to feel my presence.

I couldn't go anywhere without magic announcing I was there. Puca, too, suffered from the same affliction.

Cernunnos words vibrated out to greet me, and all turned to see why they crashed into a magical wall.

My personal wakes stopped everything.

As the crowd moved to create a pathway right to my father, I took in the blooded Fae at his feet.

The sharp green of a freshly cut emerald met mine and I narrowed my eyes.

Finian.

My left hand ached to ignite and cover him in flame. This new power over an element was a bit tougher to control than it first appeared.

I gripped my hand closed to hold back the heat before it ignited. I pulled in air through my nose and pushed it out past my lips.

My wings moved in time with my breathing. I'd rather they remain still, but wings don't work like that. They move with your chest and back muscles.

When a butterfly sits perfectly still, it's holding its breath, probably hoping you don't see them and will pass on by.

When I stood still it was similar, only I was not hoping you would pass on by. I was hoping you stopped being an ass. Otherwise, I had to display a show of power, and that may involve your death.

"My Queen," Cernunnos murmured while acknowledging my presence. He bowed his head and went through the normal motions of homage while I waited.

Board with protocol and courtly bullshit, I took in Finian. His state of being was curious. His lower legs were covered in cuts, his blue blood flowing freely down them.

Part of a shoe was missing as if it was cut off, and a long slice followed the missing piece.

Standing next to him were a group of tiny, filthy people, one of which had his back to me while he continued stabbing Finian.

"Stop!" I ordered.

The little creatures waked with bloodlust as the female next to him elbowed him.

"What? The big Fae said we could." It was a whine and a retort at the same time.

"The Queen said stop, clod brain." The female remarked, and smackedthe back of the male's head.

He whipped around to retaliate.

"If you land that blow I'll turn you to ashes where you stand."

The male's hand froze midair. His tiny eyes grew to the size of walnuts as he turned to take me in. His mouth formed the shape of an O.

The female kicked the back of one of his knees and he crumpled to the ground.

"Kara," he growled.

"Shut up, you fool! She said she'd kill you." The female crossed her arms and stared him down. After that, she uncrossed her arms and looked up at me, touching her grimy index finger to the bottom of her chin, an attempt at a clumsy curtsy. Tottering, as her body lowered on weak knees, she blinked and smiled, revealing the only clean part of her body — teeth.

For the first time in weeks, I wanted to smile. Kara and her complete lack of guile cut the tension like butter. The crowd around me snickered.

I couldn't laugh. I didn't want to insult her. Her aura waked with pride and leadership. It would undermine her position in her band of tiny dirty cretins.

She didn't bother with the Fae signs of respect. She believed we were on equal ground. Size aside, to meet anyone as an equal was refreshing.

"I am Kara, Queen of the Brownies," she announced, tilting her head up and smoothing her matted hair back from her face.

No one moved or replied. Her eyes narrowed, and she growled at her gathered menagerie of followers, then she kicked the man on the ground in the back.

"All hail Queen Kara!" The man called to the other grimy members. They repeated the mantra back to Kara, and she shined with pride.

Finian chuckled at the show. As a response, Kara whipped around and stabbed him in the big toe.

"Shut your traitorous mouth, fiend!" She yelled. She then bent down and picked up a clod of dirt and chucked it at his face, beaning him in the eye.

However amusing I found the band of brownies and their fearless leader, my quest for Janice and Jacques couldn't wait.

"Queen Kara?" I asked.

She turned and smiled up at me with her gleaming teeth. "Didn't think us, the smaller Fae, could catch a big one, did you?" pride swelled in her breast, and I didn't want to burst her bubble.

Finian was clever but not a great fighter.

"I never thought much about it," I replied, leaving out the part where I didn't know they existed.

"Puca told me to keep an eye out for a couple big ones lookin' for a way out. You must be Sarinha, the big Fae Queen." Her smile broadened. "It is a pleasure to make your acquaintance," she remarked, tilting her head in acknowledgment and lowering her eyes.

I smothered a smirk with the reality that every moment equaled hours on the surface. "We will take the prisoner from here," I stated.

Kara dusted her hands off. "Come on, we gotta keep lookin' for the other traitors. Fae has no use for those that turn their backs on us." She nodded at me as she herded her band of dirty away.

No thanks were requested, nor did I offer. She'd done her part, and now it was time for mine.

In a flash, I was at Finian's side and slammed my foot into his chest. The impact landed him flat on his back with his hand caught underneath him.

"What have you learned?" I demanded.

Cernunnos drew in a breath and pushed it back out. "Jacques is on the surface."

This, I already knew and hadn't shared with anyone.

"The trail was a decoy. There is a sinkhole in Fae that leads to the surface. A round and a song will free you from the Hallowed Hills." He nudged Finian's face to force him to look up at his betters.

Finian, unlike Deston, was never a Prince. He was only a grasping Fae, hoping for a higher standing. His compulsion lingered in the air. He was trying to use it on Cernunnos.

I released a bitter chuckle.

"You think you can influence the outcome of this meeting?" I shook my head. My left hand throbbed with heat. My desire to burn the truth out of him ached within me.

Finian's head lowered, as did his attempt to compel Cernunnos. His eyes grew at the sight of my glowing hand. The skin resembled the blackened skin of the lava lake with cracks of orange-red shining through the cracks.

It looked more like the skin of Ignis before I stabbed her.

My left hand had taken on the form of elemental fire. I spread my fingers in front of his face. His saucer-shaped eyes tracked the movement, his brows crinkled with fear. He coward away from my hand.

In a survival situation, it is normal to back away from the object of your fear. I'd been there and understood that reaction. Only for Finian, it only moved him closer to my quicksilver blade. I firmly held the blade in my right hand, touching the ground next to him.

I raised the blade and placed it gently on his shoulder. With a fiery finger, I pushed his chin up, and he screamed in pain. An excitement I'd only recently become aware of flooded my system.

The hunt.

It worked like adrenaline and serotonin wrapped up with a hint of caffeine. It gave you pleasure, energy, and the power to make anything happen.

I loved the taste. It was an addictive power. I should rein it in and work to keep control. Instead, the vision of Janice after I pulled him from the iron room Jacques and Deston threw him in clouded my thoughts.

The flesh around Finian's chin blackened and flaked away.

"Where is Jacques on the surface?" I opened my stance, keeping my body light and ready for a fight. The snap of my fingers released his bonds. It freed him to fight me.

That was what I wanted - the fight.

"He's searching for Pil," Finian coughed. I removed my finger from under his chin. His lips were swollen, and a small portion of the skin covering his chin flaked away, revealing the bone underneath.

Finian's eyes welled with tears.

I leaned in. There were no walls here to record my words or deeds. I wanted him to know the most powerful weapon in Jacques arsenal was gone.

"She's dead," I whispered. My lips curled back in a smirk before filling out to a full-blown smile.

He retorted, "Not all of her. I saw Arthur and Pil's child."

Before he could say another word, I chopped off one of his arms, then used my hand to cauterize the wound. The screaming was blood-curdling.

He fell on the stump where an arm once hung. His face was half in the dirt. The tears from his eyes were mixed with the soil, turning his face muddy.

"Where is Jacques?" I screamed and raised my sword.

"They will bleed Nick dry and use him to make more—

"

My blade was down, and another of Finian's body parts lay on the ground next to the shrieking torso. I followed up with a hard burn to seal the wound and keep him from bleeding out too soon.

My fear for Nick hit me full force. "Wrong fucking answer!" I yelled. "Spread him out!" I shouted to Cernunnos. He and Mod pulled Finian's legs from under him and held them wide away from his body.

I was trying to decide which leg I wanted to take next, when a disturbance in the magic waked down from the top of the hill.

CHAPTER 29

MERCIA

There were no words to describe how I felt. Alice didn't ask. Unlike her father, she wasn't a talker. She did use the word curious more than necessary.

My blood burned with the need for the hunt. It was an unquenchable fire, and it waked over me. I needed to kill every witch in that city. The vision of bright green flames raging over water occupied my every thought.

If I kept dreaming about what I was going to do when I got back to the surface, then I didn't think about Nick.

"You can't go there," Alice remarked.

"Go where?" I knew what she meant.

"The dark place where everyone dies." She stopped fiddling with my hair. I didn't look at her in the mirror. The only thing I could see was Nick's naked body slumping to the floor with the red feathery dart sticking out of his chest.

My throat closed. He'd said *'go'*. He wanted me to leave him behind. In his mind, the bowl was more important than him.

"I am my mother's daughter. I was born to the dark place where everyone dies," I replied in a dry, emotionless voice. "You should tell your daughter to stay out of my way. I have a hunt, and nothing or no one will stand against me."

Alice had dressed me in flower petals and babies' breath. It was the dress of a fairy princess. I wanted to rip every pretty flower from my body. My feet were encased in a substance I couldn't identify, and all of it made me itch.

"Stop trying to dress me up like a pretty doll. I have never been a little girl. I am not like you or your daughter. I am more Fae than human." The low growl that filled the room was my voice.

"You sound like your mother. She was the same way after your dad died." Alice blinked at me with her innocent blue eyes. She was a very deceptive Fae. She looked human, her ears barely edged in a point. It was her wit that revealed who she really was.

Her ability to weave words rivaled her father's. No wonder Puca sent her to deal with me.

She was supposed to keep me distracted with questions about my parents. That was a big fail. All the questions I had about my parents couldn't be answered by the daughter of Oberon.

"You look like Arty. Did you know that?"

Just the fact that she felt it necessary to state that fact irritated me even more.

I surveyed the room for any sign of the belt I'd arrived with. That belt still had one knife. The room was bare of anything useful.

There were creature comforts in abundance, soft fluffy pillows, and warm blankets.

I bet if I inspected the bed, it would be feathered down.

A nostril curled up in anger. The Fae down here were soft.

No wonder Jacques wants to take over.

I shook that idea away. Jacques was the problem, not a solution.

"Where are my weapons? Where is Puca Oberon?" I demanded without replying to her statement.

She indicated the door. I waited for her to go first. She giggled at me.

First rule - never go first.

She led me downstairs and into the sitting room where I'd arrived. Sitting in a pixie-wingback chair was the one time Seelie King, Oberon.

I lowered down to one knee and crossed my left arm over my chest before crossing my fingers.

"Master." I touched my fingers to my forehead and stood up. That was all the formality he was going to get from me.

"My son." He framed it as a statement and not a question.

The words wouldn't come. I shook my head.

"You will tell me what happened. I can see something of import has transpired." The leather covering his legs squeaked as he uncrossed them. The muscles in his chest tensed, and his skin rippled.

"I have wasted enough time in this realm. I have to go back for Nick right now," I stated.

"Not until you explain your markings." Puca's skin shivered. It was the first sign of an impending change.

"The human mutts are using bone-marrow transplants to create new witches. I allowed them to capture me for experimentation. They injected me with Nick's marrow."

Alice gasped and whimpered.

"Alice, go and tell Sarinha!" He ordered. He thrust his open hand out. Magic wakes erupted from the palm and ripped a portal in the room. Alice disappeared into the space on the other side.

Puca closed his hand, cutting off the flow of magic. A moment later, the portal slammed shut.

He leaned forward, "Start at the beginning and leave no stone unturned."

His instructions bounced off my psyche, my lips moved, regaling him with the tail. My mind, on the other hand, didn't give a hoot.

He never spoke a word even when I told him Nick changed to a wolf.

The vision of Nick falling in that tunnel played over. I didn't bother to respond to Puca's next inquiry. I thrust my hand out with my fingers splayed wide.

Magic blasted from my palm to the flowered sofa. The air tore into a thousand wakes, each rippling away from the portal. Just beyond the rippling opening was the tunnel.

"Stop!" Puca shouted.

The portal closed, and I fell back, landing hard on my ass.

"Mercia, you are not prepared to fight an entire city. Nick will survive. Without the practice of a song, even the strongest Fae will die in battle."

I blinked up at the Fae in control of my life and Nick's future.

"I opened a portal," I whispered.

"You did, hunter. This is an interesting twist in the war. You said Nicolas changed into a wolf?" Puca offered me a hand up.

I took it only because of the truth of his words. I was dressed like fairy Barbie, not G.I. Joe.

"I could decimate that city without even one weapon," I remarked to save face.

"Little one, the only spell capable of laying that city to waste would kill everyone. Is that your intent?" He stared me down with his hard canary yellow eyes.

I looked away, "No, not everyone there needs to die."

Ring around the roses was only appropriate for a battlefield where the enemy is clear. My firsthand knowledge of that song was seared in my memory.

"Your work on the surface isn't done. I can't have you racing after my son."

I opened my mouth to protest—

"You will have your leave to do as you please after you retrieve the rest of the wand of Danu," he ordered. The magic of the oath wrapped around my neck tight, forcing me to obey.

I gritted out, "Yes, master."

A devilish grin scraped across Puca's face. He shuffled around behind me. "With the ability to open a portal, Sarinha cannot stop you from crossing the realms," he whispered over my shoulder. "You can go where the hunt takes you, little one," he chuckled with glee.

My eyes widened.

Ron, Nick, and all the kids.

I could get them all and none be the wiser.

Puca chased around me a few times. A picture was forming of him. He danced when a plan was going well. He thought he was clever.

Puca didn't plan this, but it couldn't have worked out better for both of us.

"Do you have any idea where the other half of the wand of Danu is?" Puca asked a moment before he shivered and wiggled his nose.

"Yes, Master. I do," I remarked, then I thought again, "Do I need the dress?"

"Not unless you believe it will work in your favor." He shrugged and slicked his curls back.

"Then why did you put me in it?" I scoffed with a snarl.

"Fae like pretty." He stuck his lower lip out in a pout. He kissed both my cheeks.

I rolled my eyes and used my newfound power to open a portal to CB 784.

"You can never go home again, Mercia," Puca drolled.

"That is a lesson I've already learned. One last thing, in case I don't make it back. A Fae named Finian is helping the Govs. He visited the New Orleans Coven. I think he made me." A breeze rolled off the Willamette River, carrying the clean scent of pine.

Puca whispered over my shoulder, "Why do you say that?"

"Because I repeated part of Momma's mantra." It was a big fuck up, but I wasn't going to stay hidden forever. Even Momma couldn't hide in the end.

"What part?"

"*I never give up. I am the predator. All else is prey.*"

Humph was the only sound he made. "At least you didn't give him all of it," he remarked, then snapped his fingers, replacing the horrid dress with a leather jacket and breeks. The belt I'd returned with was once again around my waist.

"Do you need a quicksilver?"

"No, Cassidy has everything I want." I lept through the portal and into the octopus room, releasing the magic.

I expected the CB to be empty, and it was. Other than a few wrappers from food before the fall, the giant a/c system that once provided cool air to this building was vacant.

My old rooms had weapons galore and a trap.

I'm sure of that.

I hummed a protection bubble over my skin and hopped into the vent heading for CC. That was the last place I'd seen my crossbow.

Singing *Jack be nimble* and *light as a feather,* I worked my way through the duct system.

The vents faced down in every room. My duct was square, an intake vent, as the outtakes were round. The duct system was pretty simple, and the metal walls had pictures scratched into them at junctions telling which way to go.

I followed all the pictures that looked like a TV from before the fall. That was Cassidy's domain. That was where the answers would be if there were any to be had.

The vent outside the main door to CC revealed not a soul. Part of me hoped I could kill someone. The anger over Cassidy's betrayal lingered not just in my mind but the buildings.

The wakes around the door to CC were innocuous. Rather than chance it, I moved on to the antechamber.

The room looked much the same as it did when I was last there. The stand they had me bound to still stood off to one side. A belt I'd once worn lay over the back of a chair.

The room looked like it had been abandoned almost right after they removed me. There was a blood spot on the floor, but it was not big enough for someone to have died. It was a survivable injury worth of blood.

My lungs expanded as I pulled air out of the room and over my olfactories. The smells were stale.

No one's been here, not for a while.

Why would Cassidy abandon his CB? Larka said she would give him the city. But he failed. He turned me over, and I got away. That didn't sound like it deserved a big payday.

This CB was one of the nicest in the city.

It's a trap.

Of course, it was a trap.

Why wouldn't it be?

They thought that I would come back for something.

Ron maybe?

If so, why wasn't Ron there? Why not have him where I could see him?

Because Cassidy didn't have Ron, but he was supposed to catch me.

The only thing he might have is my crossbow.

I didn't carry it on purpose for years to make it look like it wasn't important. I left it on the wall out where anyone could see it as proof.

No one knew it was my mothers, except Jacques. Only because he gave it to her. Jacques is trapped by Wyld, so no worries there.

That Finian guy might know, if he saw it.

The magic surrounding the bow was unmistakable. Jacques' magic shined like silver.

Momma said so, so it must be true.

I unclipped the vent cover and lowered my head through the opening. The room waked with the normal tunes of whatever material things were made of. The plexiglass window that divided the CC room from this one was still intact, with a few new scratches.

I stare through the glass at the chair in the center of the room. The chair was positioned facing out for all to see and held the one thing I wanted, the one thing I needed.

Momma's crossbow.

The hole in my belly began to churn. My imaginary pixies were hungry, and magic didn't have a conscience or a plan.

No matter how much I wanted to stay in the air duct, I couldn't. My actions were not my own. My body repositions with my feet at the edge of the vent opening.

"Someone is here."

I recognized that voice.

"That'sss, not poss-ssible."

That voice, too, was familiar. The magic pulled at me to retrieve the crossbow. My jaw locked down on the grinding pain in my belly as I held back.

"Would you shut the fuck up, you lisping piece of shit. If I tell you someone is here, they are. It's Mercia. I know it is." Cassidy sounded angry.

"That cunt issssn't going to come back here," Tipup hissed.

Part of me wanted to snicker. The other part wished I still had his front tooth to mock him with.

A plan formed in my mind, a plan that magic would be satisfied with. I took a deep breath and pushed through the vent, landing on my feet between the warlock and the dipshit.

I hummed *come back peter, come back paul* and pulled the weapons from their bodies.

"Mercia…" was all Cassidy got out before I kicked him in the stomach, knocking all the wind out of him.

I whistled and slammed Tipup against the plexiglass wall. The surface cracked under the pressure of the magical push. Extending my hand, I opened my palm and a portal ripped the surface next to Tipup.

The scene beyond was a spire from the Cathedral Bridge. I released him from the wall and watched as he fell into the portal and down the side of the bridge's support.

A smirk scraped over half my face.

"You stupid changeling!" Cassidy yelled as his fist collided with the side of my head.

I lost focus, and the portal closed with a snap. I never got to see Tipup's splat on the water.

The blow turned my head, forcing me to look at Cassidy.

"Larka was right. She said you'd be back for that crappy bow." Cassidy was always good at the bullshit game. It was the most Fae part of him.

The word games were his forte, and he loved to play. It gave him a sense of power.

"Still think Larka is in charge? Still think you're going to get what you want? You stupid fool! You're as dumb as a Fomorian minus the smell," I chuckled at him.

He dodged right, and I cross-stepped left, countering his move. He opened his mouth to sing, and I throat-punched him. Cassidy choked on the pain and doubled over.

I raised my knee to meet his face, my elbow at the ready. Cassidy, too, raised his opposite leg and leaned into me, throwing us both off balance.

I landed hard on the floor with Cassidy following a moment later to push all the air out of my chest.

"You little Fae bitch," Cassidy coughed, one hand gripping his neck while the other hand was curled around my throat.

His green eyes gleamed with malice. I could sense the same lust I'd seen in Dr. Chock. He enjoyed dominating me.

"It's time you bowed to your warlock. I own you." He pulled on my leather breeks.

My hands scrambled at the grip around my throat. I couldn't pull in enough air to hum. The pressure grew in my chest. I kicked my legs to keep him from pulling my pants down.

I was slipping away. Cassidy had to let me breathe. He wasn't going to kill me. Not after all these years. I was his unicorn, not that he understood what a unicorn really was.

Or how they lure you into killing you.

I had to wait for my chance.

He rolled me over, releasing my throat. I coughed as air, sweet air flooded my lungs. He had me trapped between his legs. He leaned back and pulled my pants down to my knees.

"Oh god, you have a sweet ass." He rubbed a hand over my bare skin, then slapped a cheek.

The rush I usually felt with a slap only grew as he slapped the other cheek. I sang for Jack to be quick.

The jolt from my magical hit raced through my body. My hands planted on the floor, and I pushed back, throwing him off. I snapped my breeks away and spun around on one knee, letting my foot meet his face.

His head snapped to the side, and bluish red blood sprayed the plexiglass wall.

I used the momentum of the kick to reach my feet. The next blow landed in the dead of my thigh, colliding with my femur bone.

I collapsed to the ground. Cassidy grabbed the back of my head, lacing his fingers into my hair. "Thank you for getting those pants out of the way. It makes it easier to fuck you," he laughed.

He still thinks he has the upper hand.

I sang for sixpence, upping my power as my elbow rammed into his gut.

He gasped over my shoulder, and his grip on my hair tightened. He retched my head back, pressing his lips over mine.

My teeth locked onto the fleshy part of his lower lip until the copper taste of blood flooded my system.

Unfortunately, I couldn't use the hunter curse with my mouth closed, so I released his bleeding lip.

He punched me in the kidney, and I whimpered in pain. I sang

"Wind the bobbin up,

Pull, pull, clap."

Cassidy punched me in the spine, and a shooting pain raced over me. However, I sang the next line,

"Wind it back again,

Pull, clap, clap"

He hit me in the side of the head.

I close my eyes to keep the spinning from stopping me.

"Shut the fuck up, you stupid bitch!" He shouted and locked his hand around my neck.

"Point to the ceiling"

The magic formed and grabbed a hold on him, crashing him into the ceiling.

I pulled in a deep unhindered breath of air.

"Point to the floor"

Cassidy's body slams into the floor at my feet.

I smirked. I couldn't help it. Cassidy deserved a good ass-kicking.

"Point to the window."

His face collided with the plexiglass, creating that satisfying crunching noise I loved. Blood trickled down the plexiglass, following the cracks Tipup made.

I sang the last verse with a little more glee thank necessary,

"Point to the door."

The metal door to the CC met Cassidy's body, and he shrieked in agony. The various bars across the door created the perfect surface to break bones.

Cassidy slid to the floor like a broken doll, his ashen face colored with a waterfall of blood pouring from his nose. He coughed and a little blood laced his lips. My smile grew. I didn't know if his lips were bloody because I bit the shit out of it or from internal bleeding.

Humming, my protection bubble locked him in place.

"I can tell you where Ron is. If you leave me be, I'll tell you."

I chuckled at his pathetic offer.

"You think I couldn't take that information if I wanted it?" With a snap, my breeks were back in place. Taking the view Cassidy was eating away.

"I don't need you for anything," I remarked.

Turning away from him, I began picking through the weapons on the floor.

"Larka doesn't need you either. They got a full-blooded Fae, and they are going to bleed him dry." A dry laugh of nonchalance issued from his mouth.

"So what? Why would I care about some random Fae?" The weapons were a sad mixture of crappy guns that misfire and dull knives.

"What about the kids from Fadmor's CB? They overran that CB and took everyone. Fadmor knew that Fae. The one Larka has."

I froze. The only Fae Fadmor knew were Puca, Nick, and me.

I whipped around to face Cassidy.

"You are lying!" I shouted as the plexiglass behind me crumbled to the ground. The space between the two rooms was no longer separated.

The magic took the opportunity to force its will. Like a moth to a flame, I was pulled to the crossbow. The pleasure I'd always felt at holding the silky smooth wood raced over me.

My free hand lifted, and I fought, gripping my fist. My brain screamed at my body to drop the crossbow and not open a portal.

Magic, like Puca, always has other plans.

I was pulled through to a section of the Hallowed Hills I'd never seen before - Wyld.

"Good, Mercia. Just in time," Puca indicated a scene in the distance.

The Fae had green gossamer wings, jet black hair, and a thorny white crown. She was standing over another Fae.

"The Queen," I breathed.

"Yes." Puca clapped his hands together. "Is that the Fae you saw in New Orleans?" He whispered in the shell of my ear just as the Queen stepped to one side.

I glimpse his face a moment before she lowered a quicksilver sword and hacked his arm off. The screaming ensued.

"Yes," I said with no emotion.

He and his kind should die in the most painful way possible.

"Good," Puca danced around me. "Have you completed your quest?"

I didn't respond. I was too busy watching the gory scene play out before me with a touch of awe. I handed Puca the wand.

"Go find Nicolas!" He ordered.

This was one order I was only too happy to execute.

CHAPTER 30

SARAH

There, standing next to Puca, was a vision of Arty. The girl looked just like him, only younger. Tears pricked my eyes.

I shook my head to clear the illusion away, and just like that, she was gone. Puca remained there, holding a wooden object that waked with the power of Danu. He moved his head down a fraction of an inch, then opened a portal and stepped through, disappearing from the scene. My nostrils flared.

Puca - always where you don't need him, never where you want him.

I stared down at Finian. His blubbering should have softened my heart. If I was still part human, it would.

I asked my question, and Finian gave me a none-answer, "Don't you want to know where Nick is?" his sniveling raked over my nerves. I took a leg and let his howls of pain ring while I closed the wound.

Cernunnos coughed.

My blood-covered hand cooked the fluid away. The scent of cooking blood was no different from the flesh.

The scene of our tete was in the hollowed depression. At the rim surrounding us stood more Fae than I'd ever seen at any one moment, even during the Wyld hunt.

I'd promised to send Finian's arms and legs to the four seasons. I couldn't stop now. Fae needed to understand the price of theft.

You steal from Fae. I steal your life.

Jacques stole from us all. He stole our peace. He stole our innocence, a thing so delicate and precious it could never be replaced.

A righteous anger raged through me.

"Where is Jacques?"

"No one can heal me. I won't be allowed to live. I have no reason to answer you," he snarled in between the panting to get past his pain.

"Revenge, you can answer for revenge. Deston would still be alive but for Jacques," I replied.

The pain etched into Finian's face dissolved into despair. "Lanta."

My blade lowered. Silver pressed through Finian's sternum just like cutting cold cream cheese. The sucking sound of a blade exiting flesh followed as I pulled out. I quickly chopped the other leg off.

"You know what I want." I turned my back on the carcass. I didn't want to look at what I'd done.

Even so, the thrill of the hunt still raced in my veins. Vitriol pooled in my mouth. Cernunnos and three other rounds rose into the air and raced away in different directions.

"You are either with me and Fae, or this is what happens to you!" I shouted.

My burning palm spread, ripping a portal into the air. I turned just enough to glance down at what was left of my seneschal. I threw the green fire of Fae over his torso and stepped into the throne room.

There, in the middle of the room, next to the effigy of Nikki, was the stone well of Danu. Wakes of magic covered it, masking its presence. There had always been a well in the throne room. Only now, it was the real one.

Puca had used Finian's death as a lightning rod to attract every Fae in the hills, pulling them away from this one spot.

I turned, and there, leaning on the stone throne, was Puca. His long legs were crossed as were his arms. The lack of shirt wasn't a shock. Yet, I heaved a sigh nevertheless.

"Well played! Finian is no more, I take it?" Puca inquired.

"You knew that was always going to be the outcome of that encounter," I groused.

"Yes, that was very helpful." He found himself clever and wanted a pat on the head.

"You have the wand?" I stated, ignoring the self-aggrandizing.

I know I didn't just imagine that.

Even if I did imagine the girl, Arty's daughter couldn't be down here. I'd never be able to let her leave. Child or not, Puca wouldn't take a chess piece like her off the board.

"I have all the vestments of Danu, save one." He pushed off the rock, pivoted and shuffled a few steps this way and then, he did some weird kickball change and pivoted again.

I waited for him to fill me in on the last part. He didn't.

I huffed. "What are we missing?" I asked.

"A song." Mom's high sweet voice enveloped me. "You need the right song to open the stones."

Puca pretended to shoot a finger at her and winked. A shimmer of pride settled over him.

Ugh!

"Mom, did you ever open the stones?" I asked to find out just another piece of my mom puzzle.

"No, but my mother did." The words died on her lips. Her blue eyes grew in shocked wonder. "I think I know where the song is," she whispered.

"Alice, don't say another word," Puca growled. The flesh of his chest rippled, and fur began to cover his body.

Mom glanced from me to him, then bit her lip.

"We should go," Puca barked with saliva dripping from his sharpened teeth. He opened a portal and waved us both through.

Every step on a path takes you toward your goal. My goal was twofold. *One - save Janice and Nick. Two - end the rule of Wyld once and for all.*

That meant killing Jacques.

Opening the stone circle of Danu was a big question mark.

"What do the stones do?" I asked since Puca had to know.

"It is a portal," he remarked.

Puca had delivered us to a cave filled with the curlicue markings. They swirled into and out of each other in a beautiful fashion. All carried a faint glow.

The cave was filled with holes, each leading away from this main room.

"Where are we?" I inquired, still trying to take it all in and make sense of the scrolling designs on the walls.

"These tunnels once led to the wishing well and the stone circle," Puca replied.

He wasn't dancing now and that worried me.

"Alice, what makes you think you know where the song is?" Puca asked. Each word was carefully enunciated.

"Well, I don't know where it is, per se, but I know who would." She raised her eyebrows to emphasize the information.

I leaned in, tilting my head down. Mom always did this and I hated it. She would say something obscure then let it hang in the air forever.

"Yes, darling," Puca urged her on.

Glad I'm not the only one irritated by it.

"The Keeper's Quilt? My family's grimoire?" she supplied with a half-smile of hopeful understanding.

"I have no idea what that is. Mom, we didn't own a quilt of any kind." I rolled my eyes.

My mother lived in a dream world. I ran my hand over my face to wipe away the hope that lingered behind.

"Of course, we didn't. I left it in Ireland, where I buried the bowl," she scoffed as if I should have known this.

"That smelly lump of fabric she went back for?" Puca retorted. His canine fur had only just receded, but now it was back.

"Yeah," mom brightened, happy someone knew what she was talking about.

"Where is it?" I asked to move things along.

Time is a commodity.

"The last time I saw it, Pil had it in her bag. It was just before she left with Mercia in her arms." My mother looked down at the floor in thought. "It is curious she didn't offer it to you" she remarked to Puca.

"Alice dear, she'd touched the bowl. She was the new keeper. She understood that," he explained.

"But Pil is dead, mom."

"Mercia is the new keeper. She must have it." Mom nodded to reassure herself, or so I thought.

Because I'm anything but reassured.

Puca smoothed her blond hair back from her face. "Pil never showed it to me. How can you be sure the quilt matters? Stop with your games."

Her lips pierced to the side as her eyes narrowed. A clever gleam flooded her face.

"The quilt carries a song. Demelza said it could change worlds."

I groaned. First of all, calling her mom by her first name bothered me. Secondly, my mother was as bad as Puca when it came to subterfuge. Her dumb-as-a-box-ofrocks was an act.

Why haven't I seen that?

Maybe I didn't want to see it. Everybody that ever knew her believed in her innocence, including me. And that had protected her.

"So, where is it?" I asked, ignoring her devilish smile.

"Mercia will know," she replied.

Puca stabbed me with his golden eyes. "She will come to us," he replied.

"I hope you're right," I remarked.

CHAPTER 31

Mercia

I took one last look at the Queen's back as she lowered her blade and chopped Finian's other arm off. It was a thing of beauty. The way she worked her blade, it was like an unconscious extension of her body. The wake of her magic beat with the hunt. The scent was thick in the air.

It wasn't my hunt, so the drug of it didn't pull me in. A hunter with less training wouldn't be able to turn away. Yet, I had a different prey of my own to track.

Her eyes flashed over me for a split second before I ripped a portal and jumped through. I couldn't chance her deciding to try to stop me from leaving Fae. I hadn't missed the red stoned ring on her right hand. That was one piece of Fae I never wanted to meet again.

———

Blue and red blood still coated the rough-hewn walls of the tunnel. The bodies were gone, yet the blood remained. The trail of Nick's magic was gone too.

I slammed the opened door in frustration, then I kicked at the dirt. There was nothing left here of Nick. Not a drop of blood or hair. He was gone.

I pulled my hunter's cloak and moved through the underground facility. The operating room was a disaster.

The tables were overturned, but the wake of the iron in them still reached out to burn me. I sang for the wind and pushed them to the side.

My boots crushed broken glass and hard plastic into the concrete floor. I kept moving light as a feather until I reached the safe.

It was gone, too.

The place it once occupied was now empty, save the bolts where the steel box was wretched from its seat.

There was nothing else here, and the eerie quiet seeped into my bones.

I found a set of stairs and took them as far as they would go. They ended at a door next to a window. The sight outside was nothing short of a shock.

The water that had once been held back by magic freely flooded what was left of New Orleans. The raised catwalks barely broke the water's surface.

Cats still roamed the dry areas. However, they were now free of their masters. As animals and not pets, they were trapped on the roofs and walkways, with no way to escape.

Bloated bodies in various stages of decay floated in and around the city. Blowflies swarmed like locusts, devouring the human feast. The scent of death lingered in the marsh-flavored air.

The only way to judge how much time had passed was the state of the bodies, and the age of the char-marked buildings.

The scorch marks were old. Whoever did this burned many of the buildings. The smoke was long gone, and there wasn't a cinder to be had anywhere. The city was cold.

This happened weeks ago.

Without a magic trail to follow or a song to trace, I was as dead in the water as those bodies.

I sang for the flittermice. My nocturnal friends came crowing with delight. The young and the old spoke of the desolation of the evil witches, about how a Fae with silver eyes came and bled them all dry.

They didn't see what I saw. Yeah, the witches were dead, but so were the humans. Humans that never had a chance to run or even see it coming. At least, they were entranced. The end came as painlessly as one could hope for.

Momma once said that if you sit by a river long enough, the bodies of your enemies will float past you.

She left out all the bodies that joined them in collateral damage. The hunter in me seethed for a chance to kill. Yet, the part of me that was human and still so fresh in my mind mourned all those needless deaths.

The eternal question of whether I was an aggressive assassin or a passive warrior had raged. By killing none, another came and killed them all.

If I had only killed all the witches, the humans would be free and alive. Instead, I kept my oath and followed the edicts of my master.

I sang for *Georgie porgie, pudding, and pie*. What was left of the human population exited the buildings. Cats joined them, wrapping around legs and yowling for food.

I sang for the hunter's vine to create boats and called on the gators to ferry them all to dry land. This city was dead, and they would be too if they didn't leave.

When the last of the boats were loaded, I ripped a portal and stepped into the CC of CB 784.

Cassidy lay on his side emaciated. The taste of death surrounded him. His face flattened against the floor like paint that spilled and dried.

"Sit up!" I ordered.

His eyes pulled back with some effort. "So you came back. For me?" a tired smile cracked his face. He didn't move.

I sang for sixpence to give him a little pep. His body jetted into an upright sitting position with wide eyes and shaking hands.

"That's a good one. I'll have to remember that one," he chuckled. It was weak, but it was good enough for me.

"Where did they take Ron?" This was a dance. Cassidy loved the dance.

I didn't want him to know about Nick or the other Fae roaming the surface. We were multiplying at an alarming rate.

"Larka has him. He's her leverage against you." With a shaky hand, he ran his fingers through his hair. "I'll tell you everything if you let me out of here." He looked up at me with his grimy face and twinkling eyes.

This part was never Cassidy's forte. The deal was struck, but he never sealed anything with an oath. I found it interesting. Every changeling I'd encountered understood the need to swear on some level, that the magic would hold you to your word.

"Swear to never tell another lie," I remarked and leaned back against the wall next to the stand where he and Larka had tortured me.

"Is that all? Fine, I'll never tell another lie," he drolled and rolled his eyes.

"That is not good enough." I moved and crouched down next to his bubble. Our eyes were on the same level, and I allowed a smirk to curl one side of my face. "You have to do it right."

He shrugged. "I swear to never tell a lie."

I ignored his feeble words and supplied my own. "I, Cassidy, warlock to CB 784, swear to never tell another living creature a lie for any reason."

The smooth skin on his forehead creased in understanding. To never be able to tell a lie could be a death sentence. It meant not speaking at all. Better to have your tongue cut out. At least then, no one would bother to ask you anything.

A full smile covered my face as I nodded my head to urge him along.

"You don't want to die here in that bubble, do you?" I asked and used the tip of a finger dagger to poke the sole of his shoe.

He smacked his lips together as if he needed water to form the words. I tossed him my water skin and waited while he wet his whistle. He kept the skin, hugging it close to his body.

"I, Cassidy, warlock of CB 784, swear to not tell another lie." That oath worked, and the magic swirled around us.

I wagged a finger at him. "Not good enough. Do I need to repeat myself, or should I leave?" I asked with a cocked eyebrow.

He started again and repeated the exact words I'd asked for. The magic curled around us, locking him into his world where only the truth resides.

I took to my full height. I wanted to tower over him.

"Where are Ron and the other children?"

"Lanta! Larka has them in Lanta."

I cursed under my breath. I'd been there a long time ago when I was young and fresh to the hunt. It was Momma's first stop on her revenge-fueled war-path.

I thrust my hand out and ripped a portal into the fabric of the room.

"You know I wasn't born a warlock," he remarked.

I froze and turned slightly to take him in.

"I was a human kid, completely normal. Well, as normal as a kid with leukemia can be. You have no idea how it sucks to be young and too sick to live." He looked away from me as if reliving those memories from another time.

"I should care because?"

"I got a bone marrow transplant from a donor. Then the Fae came and the fall. It happened the day before." He laughed, "Timing, it's all about timing. If my surgery had been scheduled for one day later, I'd be dead."

Cassidy looked up at me. The reality of his world hit him hard, and now he was hoping for redemption. At least that was my guess.

My body angled to face him, and I crossed my arms, waiting for the punchline to this confession.

"I woke up a couple days later in pain. The machines were on, but everyone was gone. I couldn't walk, so I drug myself around until I found some drugs for the pain."

The surrounding wakes tasted of fear and hopelessness.

He thinks I'm going to kill him.

I mentally shook my head.

"So what?" I remarked so he could keep going and get to the point.

"I loved to sing and went to the roof of the hospital as the sun rose to do just that. It changed me. I started to make things happen. It was the bone marrow. Don't you see?" he was on his knees, almost begging.

Yuck! That was one human trait the world could do without. For the love of Danu, get some self-respect!

He puffed his lips and gave me his best smolder. His intent was for me to like it. The days of me liking Cassidy were long over. After Nick, I wouldn't look at another Fae or warlock without comparing them.

"I wanted to be a rock star. You've heard me sing. I'm pretty good."

I didn't give him the satisfaction of a reply. I just waited.

He slicked his white hair back from his face, "The music changed me, and I was able to take over CB 784. The rest you know. People started calling me a warlock. I liked it."

Ugh!

He really was pathetic with his need to be understood. Absolution was for the religious before the fall.

"If your story is true, you'd be 70 years old," I replied.

"Yeah, I guess magic keeps you young longer. I never told anyone about my past, not until Larka. She was human and wanted more. She asked me how to become a witch."

Now I was finally interested in his walk down sad and pathetic land. The rest was bullshit, but this was important.

"Yeah, so you told her. So what?" I shrugged like I already knew all about it.

"She worked for the CDC. She came to Portland looking for you. They wanted a Fae specimen to study. They knew there was a Fae in the US hunting Government agents. She enlisted me to keep an eye out for changelings and anyone with too much magic."

I swallowed. I shouldn't have. It's a tell, and I didn't want to give anything away.

He began to laugh hysterically. "But they don't need you anymore. They have your little friend - Nick."

I stopped breathing as fear swirled around my stomach like a snake squeezing the life out of its prey.

"Larka is going to bleed him dry, then she'll come looking for—"

I snapped.

Suddenly a bolt from my crossbow lodged in his throat. The tenor of his laughter choked on the blood flooding his mouth, the big mouth that had always made me so angry.

Now, no words could issue forth.

The fletching of my bolt stuck out between his lips, tickling the tip of his nose. I stared down into his eyes as the light of Fae slowly dripped away.

"No, they won't," I growled.

I pulled open a portal and stepped into the Queen's throne room. She didn't even look surprised to see me.

The CDC was a dangerous place. I couldn't go alone. She would need to see reason.

The end

TEMPEST OF FAE

She was terrific, her black hair flowed behind her while her white thorny crown reached for the sky. and her golden eyes burned like a solar flare.

That wasn't what scared me, no, it was her clarity of understanding. She got it, on a level most creatures don't understand.

I swallowed back my fear. She may be Queen but my father and mother stood up to her. She will listen to reason.

I hope.

I want to bite my lip, but *they* are watching. The Fae.

I don't know if they know who I am, but they know what I am, changeling, halfbreed, hunter.

Puca, made me swear, and I am now his weapon. My mother was his too. I am her child in every way.

I will fight and kill to end this Human/Fae war.

If you've enjoyed what you've read here please give it a little love and leave a review and feel free to follow me on Amazon Or follow me on Instagram @s.l.mason_author

For the most up to date information on the Killing Gods Universe or These Hallowed Hills visit:

Quickquillpublishing.com

KILLING GODS

<u>ALETHEA</u>

We are not Gods. No matter what Zeus thinks.

Herathina

Log Entry ATD 1,784,652.51 Terra

The study of evolution had come to a standstill when we discovered Terra. It was the perfect incubator for a Millennial Project. But from the beginning, everything has gone wrong.

Our mandate said limited contact, not domination but Poseidon is too blinded by his lust for that human to listen.

Sydney

present day

My dreams are filled with an island of blue and a woman's indiscernible pleas. On the back of the dreams come abilities. Abilities I'm desperate to hide.

But it's the voice, in my mind that terrifies me most. Is it real or have I cracked? Can you live a normal life if you aren't?

Where is the island, who is the voice in my mind, what does the woman want, and how do I hide the truth and still appear normal on the outside?